Who rules this planet?

Orthicon

OR: THE HISTORY OF A BAD IDEA

David Perlmutter

Table of Contents

CONTENTS

EDITOR'S INTRODUCTION

The following narrative is constructed from a variety of sources, most of them previously unpublished, related to the creation, rise, and fall of the Cartoon Character Colony of Orthicon (CCCO) located on the planet of the same name in the early months of 2—-. Individually, these texts reflect the fact that while their authors were creations of the human mind, not to mention ink and paint, they show a remarkable amount of lucidity and intelligence, suggesting that the branding of their authors as "threats" to the world's children was not entirely an idle boast. Collectively, they give us a clear picture of the creation, rise, and fall of the CCCO, as well as the tensions within it, particularly the inter-party relations and the rejection of the status of "commodity" by the residents in favor of a more liberalized attitude that came to cause the downfall of the colony. Thus, these writings give us a clearer depiction of what is by far the most controversial event in real/fictional cartoon world relational history.

Long after the fact, with the fictional cartoon and real worlds more fully integrated than ever before, it is easy for us to laugh at the folly of our predecessors finding anything at fault with fictional cartoon characters, let alone attempting to exile such beings for supposedly "being a threat to the children," but we must not allow ourselves to become complacent in addressing the hidden issues that are slowly revealed in this penetrating narrative. The reasoning behind Orthicon, as well as the actions taken within it, reveal that no matter what the time and circumstances, racism, prejudice, and distrust do exist and will continue to do so where ignorance is used in place of education to make judgments and decisions. A close, thoughtful reading of these writings will immediately prove this.

The task of assembling a narrative from these varying sources was hardly easy. Given the isolation, anger, and resentment felt by many of the Orthicon residents regarding their exile from Earth, not to mention the extreme and highly casual fashion in which their rights and personal uniqueness were denied on the planet itself, it is easy to say that the writings produced during, or in relation to, this misbegotten enterprise would in all likelihood form the basis of an entire encyclopedia of narratives. Time and space limitations being what they are, I have chosen to focus on only the more extensive collections of writings, but in a way that reflects perspectives from all ages, races, classes, species, and political angles, for, given the circumstances under which they emerged, it is all the more important that they reflect that balance.

Though I have suppressed some passages and indicated in the texts specifically where material has been omitted, my intent for the most part has been to present the majority of this material as it was written. Therefore, when language is used that to some readers may seem coarse, vulgar, and violent (as it often was), please keep in mind that this language is used specifically for the purpose of historical accuracy.

Finally, I should say that I am grateful to all the participants for sharing their private writings and views with me in order to make the truth about these events fully understood for the first time. Though it was, for most of them, a very difficult period on an emotional level, they have all been more than helpful in assisting me to present these events as they should be seen. I also am grateful for the research assistance provided by my students and colleagues here at the University of the Six Cities, spread as we are over six campuses. For some odd reason, we seem to have ended up being based in the six cities whose citizens seemed to form the center of this narrative, and we certainly took advantage of the unique opportunity we have been given.

HISTORICAL CONTEXT

Across much of the 21st century, the United States of America, stuck as it was under the control of the very right-wing Republican party, had engaged in a systematic process of discrimination against residents of the country whose images and beliefs did not conform to accepted but outmoded views of White Anglo Saxon Protestant (WASP) behavior. These persecutions were the culmination of a tradition of racial and social prejudice that had long existed within the country's social and operational structures, issues that are too widespread and diverse to go into at this time. Yet one commonality existed among all these horrific examples of denied liberty: the existence of subtle and unsubtle means of outlining the uniqueness of a minority group with the intention of putting them "in their place." A quick glance at American history shows this has happened with Native Americans, African Americans, Jews, women, homosexuals, Hispanics, Middle Easterners, and, most recently, animated cartoon characters. All of these groups have been made to suffer physically, emotionally, and psychologically because the WASPs of America, who have traditionally held the majority of the country's social and political power, were unable to dealwith their uniqueness. It is with this latter group, particularly the notorious Orthicon exile project and the creation of the CCCO out of it, that our narrative here is concerned.

The presidential election of 2-—has already earned for itself the status of one of the most contentious campaigns in American history, easily engulfing the sordid conflicts that engulfed that of 2000. Amid constant allegations of improprieties on both sides, some of which were justified while others were merely conspiracies, a curious political manipulation began to emerge. Having fully exhausted the voters with constant talk of the threatof terrorism, to the point that this once potent issue had lost much of its force in American political debate, the members of the Democratic and Republican parties wisely shifted the direction of their policies elsewhere. Alas, for our purposes, they focused instead on the old Puritan fear of America's children coming to harm from the supposedly "evil" influence of the wicked witches and warlocks in the mass media; namely, the characters portrayed in animated cartoons.

The moral stance finally chosen by both sides was ultimately reflected in the choice of candidates. The Republicans, in their infinite wisdom, nominated for President a Mississippian named Saunders Mucklebackit, a former Baptist minister notorious for his fiery rhetoric and intolerance of minorities, and for Vice-President, Knickerbocker Jones, a surprisingly popular African American who had little sympathy for those of his own race, or other minorities for that matter, making him the most logical candidate to be paired with Mucklebackit. The Democrats were more cautious. For President, they selected the "white knight of the West," Edward Waverley, a man of sterling moral character but little political experience, and for Vice-President Bob Blahblah, a surprise candidate whose only experience of note as a politician was serving as Mayor of Frostbite Falls, Minnesota.

The disparities and discrepancies between the two campaigns soon became apparent. While Waverly/Blahblah was nothing but exemplary in avoiding typical charges of corruption directed at political campaigns, the Mucklebackit/Jones ticket was supremely effective only at hammering home the necessity of removing the presence and influence of animated cartoon characters from the public discourse. In speech after speech, the two men, with varying degrees of bile depending on the circumstances, repeatedly and succinctly spun variations on this theme. What right, they repeatedly implied, had these creations of the mind—and distorted and ignorant minds they were—to think that they qualified for citizenship in the American republic on the baseless grounds of meeting the entertainment needs of the children of America? Were they not, they asked rhetorically, simply poisoning these children with shameless, liberal rhetoric designed to undermine respect and toleration for the democratic institutions of the United States?

Waverley and Blahblah naturally opposed this attitude. Waverley was particularly insistent, as he put it, that his opponent's remarks constituted "a severe form of prejudice" which had "no basis in form or fact." What was needed, he continually reminded his listeners, was a form of government which did not serve to discriminate against those whose attitudes were regarded as being opposed to a conservative derived mandate of "morality," but rather one in which the nature of personality alone was paramount to determining the final worth of the members of a society.

Naturally, when election time came in November 2-—and the actual voting process commenced, the voters chose the man who was obviously the proper moral, ethical, and social choice for the job: Saunders Mucklebackit.

Having made this choice, the American people helplessly watched as yet another Republican president and his belligerent war-mongering cabinet were sworn in. Waverley and the Democrats naturally charged corruption and a total distortion of the actual voting results, but their claims were ignored and distorted by a media not willing to risk governmental intervention by besmirching the favor of the newly-elected President. Not about to allow Mucklebackit's regime to go unopposed, Waverley began a campaign as tireless as his presidential run to ensure that the rights of animated cartoon characters remained intact despite the plans of the Mucklebackit administration. Even in the face of the ultimate cartoon character expulsion and settlement on Orthicon, his resolve rarely wavered. His activities and support are alluded to in the narratives presented in this book, though we have chosen not to quote the specific references to maintain objectivity.

Having now gained the legislative control and political influence to put their desires into force, Mucklebackit and his cabinet now declared waropenly on the "Bacchanalian" influence of cartoon characters in

American society. The war cabinet, characterized by such hawkish characters as Secretary Of Defense Washington "In Charge" DeBarge, Attorney General Maximillian Matuskiwitz, and National Security Advisor Fenwick "Freak Out" Finster, would have it no other way. Securing the backing of this venture was the stalwart unflappability of the Chairman of the Joint Chiefs of Staff, John Milton Berle, a man who, unlike his two namesakes, possessed neither poetry nor a sense of humor in his heart.

The attack on the animated characters and their environs proceeded with grim determination. A variety of weaponry and tactics, from the use of chemical poisoning to full scale atomic weaponry, was employed, to little effect. Not only did the toons seem to survive these attacks on their lives, they seemed to prosper from them. They became ever more vigilant, in particular, because of a growing fear amongst them that somehow they were not wanted. (The methods used by the government and the characters' reactions to them will be elaborated upon in the course of this narrative.)

Having failed repeatedly in its efforts to destroy the characters, the government chose another tactic to, finally, deal with them. Working closely with the CIA and NASA, Washington determined that the only reasonable response was to remove the characters from their various television environments and onto a newly discovered planet, a sphere-shaped, life-sustaining area named Orthicon, located approximately two hundred light years from Earth. Such a setup would serve to rid the U.S. of its cartoons, and their influence, for good. With a budget of nearly $500 billion, the three organizations secretly developed Orthicon into a habitable community for the settlement of its soon-to-be inhabitants. Designated as the liaison between the new colony and the U.S. government was the decorated CIA agent Samson "Sam" Snead, particularly noted for his work against terrorism. It is with his diary, outlining his appointment to his position, that we begin our story...

CHAPTER ONE

It Seemed Like A Good Idea At The Time

PERSONAL DIARY OF SAM SNEAD

Deputy Director Bollocks called me into his office this morning, and knowing our often frosty relationship, I could only foresee bad news coming. I had, after all, made a perfect ass of myself at the Christmas party (or at least that's what Frances told me after I recovered my sobriety after the event).

Our routine in these things is pretty much set: I do something dumb, and he rakes me over the coals as soon as he finds out about it. Lately, I have been doing it a lot for some reason, so he's yelled at me a lot. Granted, I was a bit out of line pistol-whipping those Middle Eastern guys at the mall, but somebody's got to pay for 9/11.

Anyhow, my sense of concern was at a level unusually high for me as I negotiated, by the stairs, the three floors between Bollocks' office and my own. (The elevator wasn't working...again!) How I relished the thought of being a victim of yet another of his self-serving, sanctimonious tirades. Sweet, trustworthy, dependable Bollocks, that's what they all say about him, but they don't know the dark side: the guy capable of cowing and killing off entire anti-terrorist units if they screw up even the tiniest amount, and I was sure that he had that fate in store for me.

With steely determination and painful fear mixed in my heart, therefore, I made the approach to his door and knocked.

"Come in," was his response.

I entered and sat opposite him at his desk.

"Snead," he said, in that unctuous British accent he picked up God knows where, "we have a job for you."

I panicked inside but retained a calm exterior. Surely, I expected, this was no ordinary job he had in mind for me, but then again, it probably was. Or even less than that.

"What exactly do you mean, sir?" I enquired politely.

"Well, to be blunt, Snead, we were thinking of getting you out of the country for a while."

"This doesn't have anything to do with what I..."

"No, no, of course not. Although I will be mentally regurgitating those obscene elements of your characteristic boorishness for the remainder of my natural days, but that is neither here nor there! Are you familiar with the King Alfred Plan, Snead?"

"I believe it had something to do with transferring the blacks of the inner cities into the old World War II Prisoner Of War camps for the Japanese..." I replied.

"Well, it's along those lines, but on a considerably more complex level. You understand, of course, that President Mucklebackit was elected, in part, on his promise to do something about the current problems with the 'toons..."

"Yes, I know," I said. "I tossed a lot of money towards him for precisely that reason, and, being a good Republican, I'd never consider trying somebody else."

"He knows that, too, Sam." I knew this was serious because he called me Sam, which he isn't fond of doing unless he's under the influence. Then again, Bollocks always seems serious, even when he's joking, so it's hard to tell the difference.

"He specifically requested we give you this post, even though I had some doubt about your qualifications for the position," Bollocks continued, "and who am I to refuse the President of the United States what he desires."

"He knows about what I did...and what I do?" I asked.

"Very much so.He doesn't think anyone is more qualified in the entire civil service than you!"

"Well, what is it?" I asked.

"Not here, man!" he replied testily. "This is ultra highly exclusive information! We must discuss it in the only place where it is appropriate to be discussed: the closet."

So, we found ourselves ensconced in the closet while he relayed the information to me.

"Sam..." he said, "I congratulate you! You are to be the first consul of the Cartoon Character Colony of Orthicon."

"Wait a minute!" I replied. "What does that mean?"

"It's perfectly simple.As you know, we in the United States have been having an increasingly severe problem with television cartoon characters. These creatures were created originally to exist within the confines of thirteen to twenty-two episode cycles, per year if they lasted more than one year. Nothing more or less. The reason, of course, was that that was all that was required of them by the producers, their creators, and the network executives, the producers' employers. Now, with the expansion of cable television, online programming, and similar such trivialities, there exists a great demand for newer and more innovative forms of programs. Consequently, large numbers of characters have been created over the past three and a half decades, and these 'toons' have, of late, become a dangerously malfeasant political force in America. They are even now demanding their rights as full and equal American citizens, but we will not allow yet another minority group eat up our relief rolls and compete for jobs, health insurance, and the like with true Americans, like you and myself. The President made it perfectly clear in his inaugural address that he planned to do something about this whole thing quickly, did he not? Well, this is it."

"So cartoon characters are real?" I queried. "Not simply the products of a few unruly and disordered minds in Hollywood?"

"Of course they're real. Aren't you aware of the theory of parallel universes, Snead?"

It was getting stuffy and hot in the closet, and the most classified information had already been presented, so we adjourned to Bollocks' desk, running quickly and gasping for air like you'd expect. Once there, Bollocks continued.

"Each and every television animation program that has been produced in America since 1948, Snead, has existed in its own little...bubble, shall we say, of independent means. The characters in the programs exist within their bubbles, but they are also capable of existing outside of them, in our world. Many of them have gained considerable renown as entertainers, and political figureheads. Particularly on the left."

"I knew they were bad news. Environmentalism, I suspect?" I interjected.

"Yes, and all of those irritating, family values, love your neighbor materials that the CIA has no tolerance for."

"Couldn't we just destroy them?" I asked.

"No," he said. "First of all, that would be genocide- and the U.S. government has never stooped to that, particularly since they are still residents of this country, though not citizens. Second, they cannot be destroyed by the conventional weaponry we possess."

"Why, that's impossible! Surely..."

"We've tried everything, Snead," Bollocks was grave, "and I mean everything! Toxic chemicals in their water supplies. Mustard gas in the air. All manner of garroting, poisoning, shooting, stabbing, beating, and torturing! They can bend their bodies, pull and retract tongues and eye sockets, distort their height and weight like magic. Like alchemy. This is dangerous, Sam. These people, such as they are, will not submit to our traditional forms of destruction. Their constitutions and forms defy logic and this, combined with their athleticism and their fertile mental capabilities, make them enemies to conventional Americans. Enemies of the first order! They're a graver threat to us than the Taliban or Al-Qaeda, more than any other nation's militia, more than any of the alien races of the space-ways with which we now must negotiate space in the sky with. When they burrow themselves into our culture, our way of life, our children, they do not let go and, if they use their social and political influence to undermine every institution in the government, which they severely disrespect, than America as a whole may be lost."

"Isn't there anything we can do to stop them?"

"I'm getting to that," he said.

He pulled down a chart from the wall. It was a picture of a naked lady. He looked sheepishly at me and then pulled down another chart, a portrait of a unique-looking, orange-colored orb.

"This is Orthicon," he said. "A sub-orbital lunar projectile located approximately twenty-five million light years from Earth. The U.S. government discovered it during the Apollo missions in the 1970s, but we had to keep it a secret from the rest of the world, lest Russia found out about it, for obvious reasons. We have spent approximately thirty years terraforming..."

This was a new term to me, so I asked what it meant.

'Haven't you read any science fiction?"

"I have never been much of a reader, sir," I said.

"Well, all you need to know is that it means to make an alien planet look and feel as much like Earth as possible, and therefore, allow Earth people to settle and colonize the planet's territory!"

"What does this have to do with cartoon characters?"

"Don't get ahead of me," he replied.

He pulled down another chart. Another naked lady. Another sheepish grin. Another chart. This one was one of a strange device the likes of which I had never seen before.

"We have spent thirty years terraforming Orthicon, as I said," he continued. "In that time, we conquered the alien races living there and subjected them to our will. We constructed, for habitation on the planet, an exact replica of the city of Minneapolis, Minnesota, complete with a locally-staffed version of their great tourist attraction, the Mall of America. The cartoon characters will be transported to

Orthicon to live in this locale, in the process renouncing any citizenship claims they may have in America itself. You, as the consul, will accompany them on the space shuttle flight we will use to transport them, and you will be responsible for ensuring that their lives retain as much decorum and normalcy as what existed in their old environments in their new one, and all of our problems will be solved."

"What about the device on the chart, there?" I asked.

"Oh, that. That is the CIA-patented SuperSucker. It has the suction power of an entire army of vacuum cleaners! We intend to send agents such as yourself into the alternate universes where these infernal creatures are and use our fleet of SuperSuckers to flush them out. Each device will be linked to a common terminal located at the NASA base at Cape Canaveral, from which the characters—and you—will depart for Orthicon."

"So, Sam." He switched to a less formal tone. "Are you in?"

"Yes," I said after a moment's thought. "Yes, I am."

***

(the diary continues)

...and so, after I managed to clean the blood stains off of my suit, which had been soiled rather deeply by the aftereffects of the death of the mad Arab in the parking lot, I set off for home, excitedly waiting to tell my family the good news.

After a long time spent on the Beltway trying to get home, I finally got outside into Virginia and my beloved home town, Langston. Arriving at my two-story split level yellow colonial, I called out to see if everyone was home and wanted to talk.

Nobody was home. That was no surprise. The kids were probably just out at school or with their friends or whatever, and Frances was out shopping or something, since she didn't have a job and was keeping house most days like I wanted her to. And I had pretty much stopped caring about what that alien bastard Rodmond did with his days. I almost regret having saved him from those damnable CIA alien experiments those many years ago, and having him live with us here under the seemingly innocent guise of the avuncular friend of the family.

I did, however, possess a means to communicate with them when they were outside of my grasp, since they had either bought some of those intrusive portable personal communications devices without my knowledge, or by begging me to buy them until I just had to give in to preserve what was left of my sanity. So I went to my office and my computer and typed up the following message in an e-mail directed to them:

ATTENTION FELLOW SNEADS!

Whatever you do at the moment must be dropped at once! I have just received a commission to serve as the consul of the Cartoon Character Colony of Orthicon, a very prestigious post that I have, no doubt, earned for my tireless efforts on behalf of protecting the Republic from liberalism. Consequently, in about a month's time, we will all be departing for the planet Orthicon, where the colony will be located. Trust me, none of those crazy cartoon characters will be acting up on my watch over there.

Talk to you again tonight.

Sam Snead (a.k.a. "Dad")

Just to be safe, and in case all of them, by some miraculous turn of events, forgot to check their blasted electronic devices before they turned them off for the evening (I, myself, as you know, will have nothing to do with them because they blab too much about you in the wrong way), I printed off a copy and stuck it on the fridge to make it stick. Then I retired for the night.

***

(the diary continues...)

"You idiot!"

Heather, my "young adult" daughter (as she so styles herself now, but she's still a silly teenager to me) greeted me with these words when we met again the following morning at breakfast. As usual, she was in her hippy attire: sandals, dark colored jeans, black shirt matching her long hair, and a flowery headband holding that in place. That, and her black eyes, which darted out at me in their usual righteously angry manner, are pretty much the only indications of how we are related to each other.

"Heather," I said softly, rolling my eyes. When she first got into this liberal, hippy protest phase, I assumed that she would grow out of it with some not-so-gentle prodding on my behalf. Now that it looks like this phase is permanent, I have pretty much adjusted to her being mad at me for the rest of my life.

"What have I done this time to earn your enmity?" I asked her. "Aside from the fifty million other things I did wrong this week?"

"This," she snapped, and waved my message back into my face.

"Oh, good for you!" I said sarcastically. "Turns out you can read stuff that isn't on a computer screen! Maybe we can start getting into actual printed books soon!"

"Don't change the subject! You know what my political views are, and you took this government job just to spite me!"

"I didn't take it," I said. "I was appointed to it. If you actually read the piece of paper you blithely hold crumpled in your hand, you would see that I used the word commission, not job. One does not take commissions, one receives them..."

"You and your righty ideology!" she snapped back. "I don't know what you really had to do to get that rotten job of yours- and it's just a job, not a commission, by the way- but there wouldn't be any job like this for you to do if you weren't all a bunch of lying, backstabbing racists who can't stand the idea that there's some person- or thing, in this case- who's better than your precious white man."

"That has nothing to do with it!" I countered, hotly. 'Those creatures are a...drain on the resources of America..."

"...which you think you can get rid of by using some archaic government mechanisms to pretend that they never existed! Now you're grasping at straws by blaming the 'toons for everything bad going on in America today, when most of what's wrong is the fault of your crowd, anyway."

"You little twit!"

"Stop calling me little. I'm twenty one years old."

"But you still haven't voted, and I won't recognize you as an adult until you do!"

"Well, I won't. And you better get used to it!"

Would you two just shut up already?" That was not me or Heather, obviously. That was Frances, my wife. My pragmatic, subversively intelligent, thoughtful wife, still more fabulous looking at her age than some women are in their twenties. We married for love, sure, but politically we're total opposites. I mean, she used to be a rock-and-roll groupie, - that should tell you something. I blame her for how Heather turned out, but she blames me for turning her into what a wreck she became. The very idea!

In any event, Frances walked over and put her arms around us in an attempt at making some sort of consolation between us, even though both Heather and I knew ait would start snowing in a certain hot place down below before that miraculous event would totally and completely occur.

"Can we possibly eat one meal together without the living room turning into a war zone?" Frances asked. "It's bad enough you two have to be on opposite sides of the Continental Political Divide, but do you have to make it clear every time you come in range of each other?"

"Come on, Mom," Heather said. "It's not like the Civil War- or anything like that."

"Yeah," I added bitterly, looking over at Heather. "In those days, fathers actually had their daughters' respect. Because daughters were not interested in being disowned."

"Sure, Dad. Like Mom would actually let you do that."

"Exactly," I said. "Frances, you should know by now that most of this is just talk. And people can change, too. When they get older."

"Yeah," Heather replied. "When both of us get older, I might be the conservative one and Dad would be a Communist living in Ghana 'cause he hated the government!"

My face turned white at that idea.

"That's an appalling thought," I said softly.

"That's what I thought when I saw the idea of the CCCO," Heather said, starting up again. "Dad, why would you even think about getting involved with such a cockamamie idea?"

But, by this time, Frances had guided us both forcefully to the table.

"No more of that," she said, with that leaden forcefulness she brings into her voice whenever she really wants somebody to do something. "Sit down and eat!"

Neither Heather nor I, based on past experiences, want to go against her when she has that tone in her mouth. So we did as we were both told, for once.

***

(the diary continues)

...When I returned home that afternoon, my son did not waste a moment before he cornered me in the doorway. I looked skeptically at him, as he looked incredibly needy.

"You wanted something, son?" I asked.

He ran over, embraced me very hard, and said very loudly: "Thank you!"

You have to understand something about Simon. He is a nerd. With a capital N. The glasses, the obsessively tidy dressing, everything. This is not what I wanted in a son. Chalk this one up to Frances's fruity genes playing tag with my stolid ones again. She thinks this is because I was so strict with the kids when they were growing up that, now that they're teenagers, they act up" to get my goat. I beg to differ, of course.

Anyway, Simon, being the classical nerd that he is, is deeply into anything involving science, fiction or non-. Never cared much for the stuff myself at his age. I knew any remote mention of space was sure to start Simon's head spinning. Now it seems my wife had let the cat out of the bag and let him know that he was going to be actually living there, and now I'd never hear the end of it until we got there. And that wasn't supposed to happen for another three weeks.

" Simon!" I shouted, as he began pressing onto my clavicle, let me the go."

"Oh," he said, starting to back off. "Sorry, Dad."

I managed to pick myself off the ground, having been placed there by my son's over-infectious show of enthusiasm, and, adjusting the handkerchief in my suit pocket, continued to look at him suspiciously.

"So," I said, "I guess you know about the whole Orthicon thing now, huh?"

"Yeah," he answered, still unbelievably happy. "I mean, we're actually going to be living in space! My friends are going to be so jealous!"

"It's not what you think, son. Seriously. Orthicon is terraformed. Or at least the part of it we're going to live on it is. And it looks pretty much like Minneapolis. Nothing much more boring than that, huh?"

"Still, Dad, it's space! And us living with and learning from real-life cartoon characters, yet!"

That little comment set me a bit backwards.

"You mean you actually like those freaks of nature?" I said, stunned.

"Oh, come on, Dad. When was the last time you watched an animated TV show? The 1970s? There happen to be many interesting and entertaining characters among the television animation programs of the past few decades. Including a lot of good looking girls."

I immediately understood exactly what he was contemplating. "No!"

"Oh, yes," he countered,"and if I manage to convince one of them to be my girlfriend, or even my wife..."

"You will not" I blazed. "Especially not one of the animals!"

"Gross! No, Dad- one of the human girls."

"If you actually do manage to convince one of those painted petunias to go out with you, Simon- and in the rare event of that actually happening, by the way- I will block any and all attempts by you to marry. You're not even an adult."

"Only by the standards of American law, Dad. Space is unoccupied territory, so people can do what they want there."

"Listen carefully,Simon. Apparently, your mother failed to mention the fact that I am going to be the consul for the American government in Orthicon. That means I am in charge there, just like I am here at home, only on a national scale. Understand? I got chosen to head the CCCO project because I always run a tight ship, at work and at home. They are counting on me on me to keep those animated freaks, sickos, druggies and reprobates in line, and I'm sure that they won't think I'm doing my job if my son is cavorting with their women. So, if you have any other distorted ideas about space, cartoon characters or anything else to do with Orthicon, you can forget about them right now.

I got that message clear enough into him, because he promptly ran back upstairs to his room, crying like always does when he hasn't thought things through.

***

(the diary continues)

...It was late and I thought I could get some work done now that everyone was asleep. Unfortunately, I soon discovered that not everyone was actually asleep.

Rodmond sauntered through the door of my study just when I thought I would be alone. As he so often is, he was drunk. He was also wearing a pink flowered print dress and a wide brimmed hat to match. No surprise there.

There have been very few occasions upon which Rodmond has not advanced upon me with his predatory mind and his bewildering ability to assume about a million or so different disguises, which is about equal to the number of personalities he seems to possess. These beings all seem to have minds of their own and existences of their own, it would appear, and they all seem, in addition to Rodmond himself, to have made me the point man (or "mark", as is the trade term for the victims of his profession, as I have just discovered) for every sleazy con job his disordered mind can conceive. Do I like it, you ask? Of course, I don't. When he gets working, I usually get my dignity short-changed- along with my wallet.

Though I hate the way the guy short-changes me every chance he gets, I am rather fond of him. Granted, if he didn't have the family's backing and I'd been living alone when he came into my life, I would've busted him a long time ago. But, apparently, now, in this sensitive age, I have to livewith the jerk so that I won't hurt his feelings. Most of the time it's not just his feelings I want to hurt anyway.

He'd somehow managed to fit his awkward, big eyed, absurdly thin, melon-headed, sloe-eyed (from so much gin, perhaps?) body into the aforementioned pink dress and hat, and had begun to attract my attention by vomiting loudly on the carpet.

" Rodmond!" I shouted, leaping to my feet and pushing him into the nearest sofa. "Can't you see I just had that cleaned- from the last time you did that?"

Once I had him in the sofa, he freed one of his webbed paws from my grasp and slapped me soundly in the face with it.

"And what," I said, desperately trying to hold onto my patience, "did I do to deserve that? Other than not give you the money you wanted?"

"You mean you don't know?" he shouted, coming up to his feet again. I warned him to be silent, and he repeated the phrase in a softer tone.

"Of course I don't know!" I said softly myself. "How can I possibly know what it is if you don't tell me what it is?"

"Orthicon!" he hissed, insinuatingly.

"Frances told you, I imagine?" I said, crossing my arms.

"She did! And, as soon as she did, I immediately resolved to dress up in my best finery- vis, this little number- and get sloppy drunk at your expense!"

"You get sloppy drunk every night!" I countered. "And always it's at my expense! You never have any money of your own!"

"I'll ignore that! Sam, my friend, did you happen to recall where it was in the universe I said I was from when first you brought me here as a glorified family pet?"

"Uh....no!"

Don't tell me you forgot!"

" It was six years ago! Am I supposed to remember everything you tell me?"

"Well, remember this! Orthicon is where I came from!"

"Look, if you want to come with us, you're more than welcome to..."

"That's not it, Sam! I can't go back!"

"What do you mean, you can't go back? It's not like I'm not offering you a chance to go with us, Rodmond!"

"Well, how am I supposed to go back there and face my people being enslaved to keep you and the 'toons happy, healthy and content while they break their backs serving you?"

"They're not slaves! They have jobs! Good, well-paying jobs! That was part of the agreement to terraform the planet the American government made back in the 1970s, when they came up with the idea to send the Hispanic people there. It got turned towards the 'toons only because of the public outcry that would have been raised if we'd actually gotten around to sending the Hispanics there. But regardless, Rodmond, they all have positions, from what I hear, that they're perfectly happy with! As will you, when we finish talking!"

He gasped very loudly.

"What are you saying?" he demanded.

I hadn't expected this response. I had just assumed that I could bring it up quietly, at a time when we were alone, and he was actually sober, for once. But now there it was. I had to broach this subject sooner than expected, and I wasn't entirely ready for it. But broach it I did.

"Well, Rodmond..." I said nervously, "I'm going to be involved in some pretty serious work, being as I am going to be the consul for the American government on Orthicon. And, since I know for sure now that you're one of the actual native people of the planet-since I wasn't a hundred percent sure of that before- I'm going to need somebody to kind of be my liaison with the regular Orthiconians. You know, somebody who can help me communicate the interests of the consulate in terms and language that they can actually understand..."

"So you mean like your secretary or something?" he said in an interested tone of voice. "A liaison officer? Social director? Something along those lines?"

"Exactly," I said. Again, he surprised me. I didn't think, with his tiny alien mind, he would have been able to grasp the concept I had in mind so soon.

"How much does it pay?" he asked, returning suddenly to his typical, pragmatic attitude. I figured that he would reassume this stance sooner or later, and I was prepared to deal with him on this level.

"No more than anyone else except me," I answered. "Being consul, I'm naturally going to receive an annual six-figure salary that will be deposited into my bank account for when I return. Dollars are useless on Orthicon; we've been developing a currency that will be of common usage there once we arrive. You're not going to receive that kind of money, of course, but, as my secretary and unofficial number two man, you'll be pulling in a pretty penny yourself. Not to mention the amount of authority you'll be able to wield there, since you'd only answer to me."

"That much authority?" he said, spreading his arms like a fisherman boasting about a particularly lengthy catch.

"That much authority," I assured him, spreading my arms in exactly the same way.

"Are you sure I'm up for that?"

"Please, Rodmond." I said. "You were briefly a dictator in South America and you've held me hostage very competently any number of times. Not to mention the fact that you once made a very healthy living as the greatest dictator of them all- a wedding planner! Seriously, if I know anyone other than myself who is better at giving orders to people in an entirely serious, non-ironic manner, it would be you."

"Yeah," he said, suddenly remembering the past. "I guess I am. C'mere, you!"

And then, suddenly and expectedly, he grasped my face and gave me a full tilt kiss. The scary thing was, I kind of liked it...

THE JOURNAL OF HEATHER SNEAD

Early January 2——

All I can say here right now is: How dare he?

If a picture existed beside the dictionary definition of "arrogant" it would be my father's. He blithely assumes, being the patriarchal jester he is, that we'll just accept whatever he's doing as somehow "normal", and somehow manage to suck it up enough to present the right kind of appearances for his little glorified photo-ops he calls missions to preserve democracy. Well, not anymore, Dad. No, I can't call him that anymore! Not anymore, Sam! Yeah, that's it!

I can remember when I loved him once. Truly loved him. But most of that feeling is under the bridge now. He's made absolutely no effort to understand my point of view on anything. Of course, being a Republican, I wouldn't expect him to fully embrace anything I supported anyway. But would it kill him to try and give me some sympathy instead of lip service once in a while?

I can't think of anybody less qualified to do the kind of job he's being sent off to do. Dealing with cartoon characters requires sympathy and respect for their feelings. Likewise aliens. I should know. I've actually campaigned for the rights of the former with my friends, with them getting so abused by Hollywood and Washington and all, and I live with one of the latter. He doesn't get them, though- he's spent his whole life away and apart from them. He has no more of an understanding of how to deal with racial minorities or foreign nationalities than he did when he forced us all to live in Saudi Arabia that one time. I won't be forgetting that any time soon. Imagine treating women as poorly as that in this day and age...but I'm getting off topic here.

So now he's preening around the house like the big shot diplomat he fancies himself, certain that the American way is going to triumph over the foreign like he somehow always does. Pathetic! But I'm just going to hold my tongue for a while on this one. He's always unreasonable when he's in this overconfident phase. But just wait until he figures out what he's really dealing with. Pride goes before the fall, of course. I just hope I can help the 'toons wake up and smell the coffee before it's too late. They're just bound to be as ticked off about the whole thing as I am!

CHAPTER TWO

The Abductions

PERSONAL DIARY OF MUCK FLECKNOE

Likely written sometime in January 2——, either on board the space shuttle Expulsion 1 or in the holding Cape Canaveral holding area. The other diary/journal entries in this chapter probably originate from the same time.

Well, it looks like they got me. I don't know what happened, how we got here or what's gonna become of me once we get to Orthicon, or whatever the name of this place where we're all supposedly going is. All I know right now is that it doesn't look good for any of us who apparently aren't human.

Maybe if I review how all of this happened things might come to pass. It's pretty much all I can do here right now, anyway.

So I just got back from Christmas vacation in Cuba. I have no idea how my Mom managed it, given the fact that Americans are kind of unwelcome there, but, still, we went there. A nice change from gritty, grimy East Townsberg, especially when the winter hits. The wind blowing off the lake in winter is really uncomfortable, let me tell you!

Anyway, I was still adjusting to being home when the events that led up to what seems to be this permanent vacation from real life started.

I was walking down the street, still trying to get used to the bone-chilling cold after a week in the Caribbean, when my jaw seemed to separate itself from my face as I looked around a corner, and I had the most difficult time getting it back in place.

For what did I see on the corner but my imaginary friend, Bootylicious J. Krinklebein- "Boot" for short (look, I was only two years old when I created him, okay, so give me a break about the name!)- standing on the corner clad in a yellow stocking cap and scarf, busking- busking!- and actual seeming to do a good job at it, in spite of the fact that he has no voice and no other perceivable talents other than trying to con people out of their money. People like me, for instance.

There was a time when he and I were the best of friends. Of course, I created him because I didn't have a lot of friends in the first place-very few two year olds do, after all. The trouble was, as I've grown older and slightly more mature (at least I think), he, on the other hand, has not. He and I (or, if you are naïve enough to think that imaginary friends are not real, simply I) did raise a bit of hell, so much so that my Mom put her foot down and said I had to get rid of him. That was two years ago, when I was six. Fortunately, there just happened to be a place in town, Finster's House for Previously Utilized Imaginary Acquaintances, where he could live and be safe and I could continue hanging out with him. Things worked out, after a short period of adjustment on both of our parts. At least they seemed to-until now.

Because there he was, all 4 feet of him, entirely blue in color, with no visible parts except his eyes, mouth and hands, prepared, as I was, for the weather, but otherwise not wearing a stitch. And singing. Playing a guitar he had somehow filched. And somehow, as he always has, believing the world owes him a living and that it's only going to be a momentary lapse of time before he cashes in the cheque.

Of course, I wasn't going to let him rip off any innocent bystanders, much less myself, without letting him know how I felt about it. Politely, I waited until he had concluded his excruciatingly painful "set", and then I approached him with anger in my heart and voice.

"Boot!" I cried, to get his attention as I approached.

He had not noticed me among the crowd that had milled around him, but the crowd had thinned out enough by this time, so that he was by now able to see and hear me.

"Muck!" he exclaimed, as we had not seen each other for some time by this point. "How goes it, buddy?"

"Fine," I mumbled with gritted teeth.

"Did you enjoy Cuba?"

"Well, it was a little hot at first, but after a couple of days I started to-never mind that! What are you doing out here?"

"Whatever do you mean?" he asked plaintively, in his innocent little boy voice. He still uses it on me, even though it stopped working on me once I started school.

"I mean, why are you out here living like this? Why are you not back at Finster's like you're supposed to be?"

"Where?"

"Finster's!"

"Oh, yeah. Well, the thing is, I can't go back there. For the time being, anyway."

"Why?"

"Oh, right. You were on vacation, so you don't know."

"What do I not know?"

"That it was shelled by the government."

"What?"

He proceeded to give me his version of how things went down, seeing how, as he put it, I was uninformed on this little matter. It seemed that President Mucklebackit's "whacko" Secretary of Defense, Fenwick Finster, had freaked out when he discovered that there was an institution for imaginary friends bearing his name here in East Townsberg, the slightly less prosperous neighbor of Townsberg, on the other side of Lake McCracken. (This was how I discovered that Mr. Finster's nickname was, in fact, "Freak Out", because he had apparently done things like this more than once.) This couldn't stand, of course, particularly since he wasn't a blood relative of the proprietors- who have since become very close friends of mine- although if that had been the case, things could have gotten an awful lot worse. President Mucklebackit had been elected because he campaigned to stamp out all signs of liberalism in America, and there wasn't anything he thought was more liberal minded than a house for imaginary friends. So, with the President's backing, Finster ordered General Berle and his troops to start shelling the old Victorian mansion in town that Finster's is based out of. The friends and the management put up a terrific fight for the place, of course, but all that got them was arrested and deported to, of all places, Gary, Indiana, because they were "war criminals" who were interfering with the proper due process of the law of the land. That was where all of them were now.

"But what about you?" I insisted. "You're still here!"

"I wasn't there," he admitted.

"What do you mean, you weren't there? You just abandoned them all?"

"I most certainly did not!"

"Then how did you not get rounded up and deported to Gary like the rest of them?"

"Because I wasn't in the house when they came. I had gone to the store to get my own supply of junk food, because some people were upset about the fact that I was taking more than my share of it from the fridge. I was gone for, like, thirty minutes, and that was all it took. Everyone was gone, and the house looked like someone had shaken it like a snow globe."

"But haven't you done anything about getting everyone back from Gary?"

"Don't think I haven't thought of that. But first things first."

"What does that mean?"

"I have to raise the money I need to bribe the Defense Department so they can start considering the idea of bringing them back."

"Bribe the- Boot, that's not the way democracy is supposed to work!"

"Is it, now? Then how did Sandy Mucklebackit get his way into office? It sure wasn't because we voted for him!"

"I'm not old enough to vote! And you're a physical non-entity, so you're ineligible!"

"Physical non-entity?". He was getting belligerent, so I needed to change the subject before things got violent.

"Look, Boot," I said calmly, "that whole 'bribe the Defense Department' scheme of yours is not going to work!"

"I thought you might say that," he said rather smugly. "So I'll have to go to my backup plan now."

"Which is?"

"My, we're asking a lot of questions today, aren't we?"

"Boot!"

"All right, you impatient little wretch! Here it is!"

He opened his guitar case and handed me a sheet of paper- on which he had drawn something. Very crudely, I should say. I can draw better than he can now- since I'm older than he is!

"What is this?" I demanded as soon as I saw the drawing.

"This," he said calmly, as if talking to someone much younger than himself, "is my backup plan. Did you not hear me tell you that first time?"

"I know that," I responded. "The question is, what is it supposed to be?"

"Only the greatest club in the universe!" he shouted into my ear.

"What?" I answered. "You're crazy!"

"Why am I crazy?" he retorted. "You're crazy for not believing in me, Muck!"

"First of all," I reminded him, "you get one of these stupid ideas every day! And on the rare occasions when you actually try to make them a reality, they never work because you never even consider the amount of actual hard work you have to put in. Not to mention the fact that you totally and completely absolve yourself of all responsibility by shiftlessly handing it over to those who have no idea how to deal with it. Like me, for instance!"

"Oh, pardon me, Mr. Let's Go on An Ice Cream Soda Bender every time he can't deal!"

"I'm getting counseling for that, okay? There is no way anyone is going to give you a permit to build this thing based on this one crude drawing! Let alone help you find a contractor who would be willing to risk their health by lining the ceilings and floors with asbestos!"

"Goggles liked it. Pitched it to her before they all got pinched."

"Well, where is she? Let her help you build it, then!"

"Can't."

"Why not?"

"She's in Gary, stupid! With the others!"

"But she's not a..."

"They couldn't tell the difference! Sometimes I can't either!"

"Enough already! The point is, nobody in his right mind is going to back this thing. Like the world needs another monstrous casino sucking away the world's money from the people who actually need it!"

"I see. Castro got to ya when you were in Cuba, didn't he?"

"I never even saw...- Quit messing with me!"

"Oh, I've only just started, angel!"

" "Angel?" What are you talking abo...Oh no. You did not!"

"I did."

On many occasions in the past, Boot has felt it his obligation-nay, his duty- to abscond with money from me to finance his mad desires. When this happens, he believes he can raid my meager funds to his heart's desire. I was finally forced to relieve him of the key to my apartment I gave him when he first went to Finster's, so he could return and visit me if he wanted to prevent a reoccurrence of the burglary scenarios that had already occurred. But now he'd done it again! How?

"How in the world did you get another key?" I demanded. "And how much did you take?"

"Skeleton keys are perfectly accessible to the public, provided one has the kind of connections that I possess. And I took all of it!"

"All of it?"

"All of it! Casinos don't come cheap, Muck!"

That was it! In spite of the chill weather, I felt warm. Extremely hot, in fact. I suddenly realized what my Mom meant all of those times she said I was "boiling her blood". My own was getting pretty hot at this moment.

"You took all of my money?" I screamed. "After I specifically prohibited it?"

"Come on, buddy!" he said softly, almost pleading. "It's for a good cause. Seriously. Ten percent of all the profits goes towards a fund to get everyone back from Gary..."

"Ten percent?" I shouted. "Ten percent of a pipe dream?"

"I didn't say it would happen immediately!" he retorted, defensively.

"I have had it with you, you little blue thief!" I shouted again. "You are not worth all the pain you keep putting me through every day! Look at me! Look at me! I'm eight years old, and already I've got bags and wrinkles under my eyes! Bags and wrinkles! And it's all because you keep hounding me and harassing me to keep you in clover every time we're even remotely near each other, you rotten...no-good...cheap...horrible....son of a SEA COOK!"

This, for some reason, set him to laughing when it was supposed to shame him.

"What are you laughing about?" I blazed.

"You," he breathed between inane giggles, "called me a "son of a sea cook". Technically, you're my father, since you created me and everything, so that makes you...A SEA COOK!"

"I'll cook your sea," I threatened, stepping forward to giving him a beating. "Along with your goose!"

That was when it happened.

Pitch blackness engulfed the entire town, followed by an illumination source that wasn't coming from the normal streetlights.

"Sucking procedure commencing!" a foreign voice said.

And then, from out of nowhere, the sound of a giant vacuum cleaner rumbled in the distance. And then it began sucking up everything. Everything! People, buildings, sidewalks, cars, fire hydrants. Everything!

Boot and I took one look at the giant lights in the sky, screamed our lungs out, and started running away. But we didn't get far before both of us were sucked into a void and carried along by the vacuum along with everything else.

"Muck, I had nothing to do with this!" Boot said over the sound of the vacuum as we went in. "I swear!"

For once, I actually believed him.

PERSONAL DIARIES OF THE SUCKERPUNCH GIRLS

FLOTSAM:

The Hot Line rang about noon that day. I picked it up. It was the Mayor, and, as usual, he was in a severe state of apoplexy about something that he shouldn't have been. He explained very loudly (again, as usual) to me that he was fearful that, somehow or another, all of us in Townsberg were being spied upon by an unknown and unstoppable entity.

"What do you mean?" I asked. "Aliens?"

"Worse than that!" he answered. "The Central Intelligence Agency!"

"What does the CIA want with...?"

I stopped as soon as I realized something. The CIA couldn't have been responsible for trying to drop that atomic bomb on the city earlier that week! (Trying, because we stopped them, as we usually do, by de-activating the thing before it hit, as I said before, diary.) Or could they?

"You don't think that they...?" I asked with concern.

"I do," he said, "and I think they're trying to get us again! Things haven't been safe for any cartoon city ever since Mucklebackit got in, and that includes us."

"But how do you think they're going to attack us?" I asked.

"That's why I called you, silly." he said, almost mockingly. "Deal with it."

Suddenly, the dial tone filled my ears. I slammed the receiver down with not a little bit of frustration and readjusted the bow on top of my head as Baubles and Betterfist came towards me, attracted by the conversation.

"Problem?" Betterfist asked rhetorically.

"You bet there is!" I answered. "Why else would we get a call during the day?"

"Well, what is it?" Betterfist returned. "It better not be some minor traffic violation stuff, because I am so sick of that." She smacked her hands together .

"Those things are important, too" I reminded her stoically. "But it's not that!"

"What is it, then?" Baubles asked.

I took a deep breath and then responded:

"The CIA."

They gasped as loudly as I had when the Mayor told me.

"Didn't we just deal with them?" Betterfist asked.

"Yeah," I reminded her. "But you know how things are with bureaucrats. You push them, they push you back harder, and it gets messy."

"'Cept you can't beat them up and throw 'em in jail like you can with our enemies," Betterfist observed, as she crossed her arms and sneered. "Jerks!"

"Now, don't talk like that!" Baubles said, crossing her own arms and speaking in her most annoyingly goody two shoes tone. "We're supposed to respect the government. You told us that yourself, Flotsam."

"Repeatedly," Betterfist added, with a fair amount of her usual annoyance with me.

"Yes, I did say that," I said. "But what I need to say to you now is that you can only respect any government organization if they show you respect in return. Do you think the CIA was respecting us when they tried to kill the entire city, including us, with that heinous bomb?"

" No!" Betterfist said. "That was the last thing on their minds."

"I still can't believe it," Baubles said. "That bomb thing was a...an...isorific..."

"Isolated incident," I responded. "No, it wasn't, Baubles. Look- I know you still want to think the government understands us, but they aren't giving us any evidence that they want to anymore."

Baubles was on the verge of tears. "You're not serious." she said.

But one look from my eyes told her I was, very much so, and the joyfulness vanished from her face, at least temporarily.

"Come on!" I said. "The sooner we find what the CIA is up to and quash it, the better!"

We flew determinedly out of the windows of our room.

BAUBLES:

I was extremely devastated to hear Flotsam and Betterfist talk about the government trying to get rid of us. Of course, I knew it wasn't just us they wanted; they had, after all, targeted the whole city with that bomb. But still, I was, as Flotsam might put it, crestfallen. Sure, we'd had trouble with government law enforcement before; ,toon superheroes like us always do. But hadn't we proved how valuable we were to America and the world? Repeatedly? Why would they want to get rid of us and everyone around us if that was the case?

Anyway, we had a job to do, and I didn't want Flotsam or Betterfist to call me out for being a weeping willow again (not like they haven't cried once in a while, though) so I followed them out the window.

It wasn't too long after that, as we flew across the downtown core and back towards the suburbs, that we spotted a suspicious delivery truck and began tracking it from above. With our enhanced vision, we were able to read everything that was written on the side of the truck:

SAM'S CIA PIZZA

SO GOOD YOU'LL WANT TO KEEP IT A SECRET

DELIVERY IN 15 MINUTES....OR WE'LL KILL YOU!

WE ACCEPT ALL MAJOR CREDIT CARDS

"Some disguise," Betterfist scoffed. "They're just setting themselves up for a fall like that!"

"Not always, Flotsam countered. "Remember when you were so certain that Cosa Nostra Pizza was really a front for the Mafia- and it turned out to be a legitimate business with no connection to the Mafia whatsoever?"

"That was a one-off thing!" Betterfist answered. "My hunches usually pay off."

"When you have them," Flotsam countered cattily, as she does when she disagrees with Betterfist.

Always with the arguing. When they fight, it scares me, so initially I flinched, preparing for the worst. But then I toughened up again. I have to play peacemaker between them, because nobody expects kind, cute, little me to have a darker side to her character, so it comes as a shock to them both when I raise my voice. As I did when I growled at them without using words to break it up this time.

"If you loud-mouthed hens are finished clucking," I reminded them, "we have a suspicious vehicle to pursue!"

"Yikes!" Betterfist noted. "You're right. It's getting away!"

"Well, what are we hanging around here for?"Flotsam said. "After it!"

We continued our pursuit, and I was satisfied for having said my piece and reminded the others that I was, in fact, here alongside them. For a few moments, anyway.

BETTERFIST:

Sure, I was suspicious of the whole thing. When had the CIA decided to get into the pizza business? Hadn't they baked enough lies around the world as it was?

I voiced my plan as we got close to the van and edged into position for an attack. I would pull on the bumper and bring it to a complete stop with a tidy yank. Then, after I had ripped off the bumper, I would take out the doors and beat up any of the guys in dark glasses that made a move towards us. Then, I would shake the van clean of any of their cheap surveillance equipment and throw it into the lake...

But no! As they usually do, Flotsam and Baubles overruled me two to one.

"We don't do those sort of things unless they're necessary," Flotsam reminded me. "We don't want to get a bad reputation for being destructive and violent, now, do we?"

"No," I said, sullenly. "We don't."

"Of course not," Baubles said in a syrupy voice. Sometimes I want to smack her when she does that.

As planned, we continued pursuing the pizza delivery van as it motored through town, without making any of the deliveries it was supposed to be making. So we knew for sure now that it was a front for something. But what?

Eventually, the van made a stop at the top of the giant hill overlooking Lake McCracken at the far end of town. When it made the stop, the men in dark suits and sunglasses-natch- jumped out and started hauling equipment out of the van. The three of us crouched in the shadows until it was considered (not by me, again!) time to jump out dramatically and reveal ourselves.

"Think we lost them?" one of the men in black asked.

"Hard to tell," another one said. "They're pretty slick, you know."

"I know," the third said, who was apparently the leader. "But, with this thing, we'll be slicker than they are, for once."

It was at this point that Flotsam signaled to Baubles and me that it was time to go into action. We emerged from the bushes very quickly, as normal, our legs spread-eagled into crouches in case we needed to be on the attack.

"That's what you think." Flotsam snarled as we emerged.

The men in suits feigned surprise for a moment, as if they had not suspected in the least that we had been following them all this time. That was a charade that did not last, though.

"So," the leader of the unit said, "you found out, huh?"

"Obviously," Flotsam said. „ The question is, are you going to stop whatever you have in mind for us and our town immediately, or are we going to have to resort to force to make you do that?"

"May I remind you," the leader of the CIA group said, in a sober, snotty voice, "that the three of us are officials of the United States government, and that you will be severely charged in a court of law if you so much as..."

"Oh, shut up!" I snorted. "We've dealt with your kind before! You might be scary to us the first time, but not the fifteen hundredth!"

"So, that's the way it's gonna be, huh?" the CIA man said.

"Yep," the three of us said as one.

"Fine," he answered. "We warned you, but you seem to be deaf to our warnings..."

"Deaf?" we shouted

"Yeah," one of the other CIA men said, "it means that you were uncooperative when we told you to back off..."

"We know what it means!" Flotsam shouted. She's always the sensitive one when our collective intelligence is questioned.

"Just shut up, okay?" the CIA leader said to the man who had spoken. Then, to us, he said:

"The point is, we've come to get rid of this town, and you're in our way! So we'll have to get rid of you first if we're going to dispose of the town!"

"And how, exactly, do you propose to do that?" Flotsam said, frostily. "It's not like you have the resources to get rid of us, let alone the town."

"Guess again, chicks!" the CIA man said. And he swept the back doors of the van open to reveal...

...a vacuum cleaner.

In spite of our efforts to remain tough at that moment, it was hard for us to resist a little chuckle at their impudence at trying to get rid of us with a vacuum cleaner, though it was a chuckle we were quickly able to suppress.

"You morons!" Flotsam snapped. "Do you really think that you can stop the Suckerpunch Girls, the undisputed, super-powered, heroic champions of Townsberg, with a vacuum? You must be mad!"

"This isn't any ordinary vacuum cleaner!" the CIA man shouted. "Have you any idea what the SuperSucker 5000 is capable of?"

"Sure," Flotsam joked. "It can clean carpets all over the world in a single bound!" That set the three of us into hysterics. In spite of the fact that she has a stony exterior a lot of the time, Flotsam can be quite the wit when circumstances allow for it.

But, looking back, that was our mistake. We let our guard down, and it cost us. Along with the rest of our world.

"Suck them in," the CIA man ordered his colleagues. "I've had quite enough of their feminist bullshit."

One of the men flipped the switch. Suddenly, we curtailed our laughing as we got engulfed in hurricane force winds...that were somehow emerging from that crappy little vacuum cleaner!

"What is happening?" Flotsam demanded as the vacuum winds picked us up like dolls and began moving us towards its nozzle.

"Can't tell you now," the CIA man said as we came towards him, "but you'll find out."

Somehow or another, we made it through the nozzle of the vacuum cleaner intact. And then, everything went black for a while...

AUDIO LOG OF JANEY WICKMAN, AKA GLOBAL JUSTICE UNIT AK 47

... "Get the robot," I heard somebody say as I flew into downtown to investigate the angry mob that had gathered there.

"Yeah," another person agreed. "Somehow or another, this whole thing is her fault! I'm pretty well sure it is."

They surrounded me, hoping to tear me apart out of ignorance and violent, unresolved feelings, the way things usually do on those occasions when my name becomes mud. But I was prepared to fight them if I had to, even though it wasn't exactly something I wanted to do to my fellow residents of Trembling Town. Super villains and alien robots, definitely. But not my friends.

At least, I thought they were my friends.

If you were to come across the scene going on at that moment, you might think that I was an innocent victim- a blue-haired teenage girl with pigtails, a blue skirt, breastplate and boots, with sinewy white arms, legs and hands, who was being surrounded by threatening people wanting to take away her life...or worse! And, if you were any sort of gentlemen or social worker or some such thing, especially if you didn't actually live here, you'd immediately want to rush to my defense and save me. Wouldn't you?

I can assure you, right now, that you wouldn't need to. I may look like some innocent teenager whose back would break if you shoved her backwards over a rock, but weak I am not. My mother should know. She built me to fight against threats to myself and to the wider world, and she'd be super mad if I didn't do my job the right way.

You can probably guess by now that I didn't come into this world the way humans do, nor did I "grow up" the same way they do, either. I am a robot, and proud of it. I can balance weights that would weaken the strongest man on my pinky. I can outrun the fastest land animals, and out-fly the fastest birds. I can communicate with any alien being-in their own language, at that! I have an arsenal inside of my body that would be the envy of any regimental army. And my lasers can fry anything that crosses their path in under a second, if anyone's unlucky enough to make me well and truly mad.

But I'm not bragging.

That's because, in spite of my great gifts, and my frequent employment of them to save my town and my home doing my job, I am frequently treated like a pariah exactly because of what I am.

I have a few friends, sure. But they're about the only ones who can see behind the shiny metal robot exterior to see the girl within. I'm glad they're here, but I only wish there were more of them.

At that moment, I knew I had to be with them. They'd saved me from the scrap heap more than once in the face of the ignorance and hurtfulness of the people of the town, and I knew they would do it again if they had to.

So, as the burliest of the men leapt towards me, attempting to pull me down and destroy me, I turned on the rockets in my feet and leapt up into the air again, making them fall down into the snow-covered street.

"Shame on you!" I said angrily. "Just because things haven't been going right for a while here is no reason to make me the scapegoat for..."

"Get lost, robot!" one of the crowd shouted angrily at me. A large snowball flew through the air and hit me in the face, with others now being poised to be thrown at me. Enough of that stuff on my body and I'd short circuit and fall down to Earth, and then they'd make mincemeat of me. If I had been made of meat, that is.

There was only one thing to do. I retreated swiftly with the help of my rockets, with the snowballs aimed at me barely missing me as I left.

***

(the audio log continues)

...I finally managed to make it home with as little damage to me as possible, thank Jobs. Brat, Shelby and Puck were there, so I knew this thing was serious. Somehow, whenever they and I intersect, trouble follows. Doesn't mean that I love them as the friends they are.. Sometimes like brothers, but that's as far as I'll go. They need to learn the consequences of being too friendly with a robot, so to speak, on their own. Especially Shelby.

"Did you see what it's like out there?" I asked.

"The snow," Puck asked, "or the angry mob after your oil?" For a seven year old, he's good. "We saw both, and we got hurt by both."

"How?"

"Well," Brat said innocuously, his red hair forming an erect point, "they said it was gonna snow last night on TV, but they didn't say it was gonna be this much. They totally got it wrong..."

"She means the angry mob, you idiot."

It was at this point that Shelby interjected. He had been facing away from me, but now he turned towards me. I could see why. He looked almost disfigured, with shiners on his eyes and a split lip. I gasped in feminine horror, something I usually restrain myself from doing ('cause of my reputation for butt-kicking, don't you know), but this certainly called for it.

"Shelby!" I gasped. "What happened?"

"It was nothing, really," he returned modestly. "Some guy insulted your honor, and I gave it to him."

"Some guy?" Brat chortled, impishly. "It was, like, half the town."

"Don't forget that they called you names, too,"Puck interjected. "I never knew there were so many bad things you could say !!"

"The point is," Shelby said, "that I took one for the team, okay?"

"That is much appreciated." I walked over and patted him on the back. He would have liked more, especially since he's, like, super in love with me for some reason, and it was written all over his eyes. Mine, however, put him down again- firmly- and he backed off.

"The question is," I mused, "if I wasn't responsible for putting that liquid mercury in the drinking water- and I wasn't- then who was?"

The guys looked rather nonplussed, like they usually do. Cue my mother, all 4 feet of her. Unless you count the hair, and then it's 5 feet.

"Ah, AK 47!" she drawled in her irritating mittel Europa accent. "You have returned!"

"Of course I've 'returned', Mother." I responded. "There's nowhere in town I can be safe anymore. You know, because of the thing with the mercury..."

"I don't know where they would get that idea. You haven't been to Mercury in quite a while..."

"Not the planet, Mom! The stuff you put in thermometers. They said I put it in the drinking water..."

"You?" she asked. She tends to get caught up in her work, so she doesn't get out much. However, she should have noticed this.

"Yes, me," I said.

"And just why would they suspect you of being the culprit?" she asked, in a tone that would have made any District Attorney proud.

"I don't know," I said. "I'm just the default person- or whatever- to blame whenever something bad happens around Trembling Town. These people need a scapegoat, and I'm it."

"You're exaggerating, Janey," Brat put in. "You know we love you..."

"I mean besides you guys," I said to him. "Everybody around here is so changeable. I only wish that they could understand that just because I'm a robot doesn't mean I'm evil..."

"Stereotypes die hard," Puck said.

"Sometimes not hard enough," Shelby added. "But you have us, Janey."

"Thank you, guys," I said, sincerely, as I blushed, and artificial tears came out from my tear ducts.

That was when the lights went out, and the ground began to shake...

JOURNAL OF DENNY PENTON, AKA DENNY APPARITION

I've seen a lot of strange stuff in my life- and I'm not even an adult yet. But this whole thing had to be one of the strangest things I ever dealt with.

The whole thing started when somebody managed to find a canister of mustard gas- which my sister swears they stopped using in warfare after World War I- and broke it open in the center of town. Guess who the enlightened people of this community blamed for it- rather unjustly, I should say.

Right! This guy.

I don't know how and why they think that. It's been like that ever since my ghost powers a couple of years ago. Something happens that has the whiff of the supernatural around it happens, and I get the blame. Of course, my parents are parapsychologists- ghost hunters, in plain English- but that shouldn't be here nor there.

In this case, I wasn't even there when the mustard gas got dropped. I was at home with my pals and ghost hunting associates, Sabina and Luther, watching TV when the news team broke in with the news of the drop. Naturally, we were all completely stunned- except Luther, for some reason.

"It could have been worse," he mused as his pushed his glasses up the bridge of his dark-skinned nose. "Could have been laughing gas."

That made Sab's Goth girl blood boil, and she pulled him close to her face.

"You idiot," she snarled. "Don't you know what mustard gas is?"

"A gas....made of mustard?" I interjected aimlessly.

She dropped Luther and grabbed me instead. "Mustard gas has nothing to do with the condiment. It's a toxic form of sulphur that causes growths in the lungs if you breathe it in, and then you die..."

"Take it easy, Sab," I said. "We can just..."

"Easy?" she snarled. "We gotta stop this guy, Den'. Or girl, or whatever the hell else thing it is. This isn't like the other stuff we've dealt with. They may have threatened to conquer the world, but they didn't go around killing people to do it."

At which point, she dropped me on the ground..

"Sorry, guys," she said. "I just have a...thing about this. I had ancestors who got killed by gas..."

"...by the Nazis in the concentration camps," I finished, affectionately putting my arm on her shoulder as I stood up again. "I know, Sab'."

"But you are correct about the fact that we need to stop him," Luther added. "If whoever that is has a full supply of that gas..."

We all shivered inside at that thought.

***

Fast forward to me, in my ghost/superhero mode, chasing a thuggish looking guy holding a canister of mustard gas, with Sab' and Luther on my heels. We'd staked out the downtown that night, hoping Mr. Lung Infector would make a return appearance. Sure enough, he did, although there weren't anybody there but us chickens...

Wait. That didn't come out right...

Anyway, I faded out, made myself transparent, entered the guy's body, and made him sit down with the canister in his hands. When I exited, I called for Sab' and Luther to tie the guy's legs up with the rope they brought with them, which they did. We removed the canister from his hands.

"Who are you?" I demanded in my heroic identity. "And what do you want..."

"I don't have to tell you anything!" he snarled.

I knew I'd have to scare him to get him to talk, being a ghostly being and all. So I split myself into five, and shouted the question again.

"Stop!" he shouted. "I'll talk! Just don't hurt me!"

"We can't promise that." Sab' growled at him angrily.

"Never mind that right now," I said to her. "If he knows where the guy with the gas is..."

"I am the guy with the gas."

So he told us. He was, of all things, an agent for the CIA. He'd been specifically ordered to destroy our community, on the grounds of us being labeled "animated cartoon characters" (Huh?) who needed to be eliminated. Turned out there were guys like him operating all over America, trying to destroy communities like ours for supposedly wrecking the youth of America.

"You're nuts," I declared. "We're not..."

"Don't take it out on me," he insisted. "I was just following orders..."

"So were the Nazis!" Sab' roared. She would have done some damage on the guy right then and there, when, suddenly, he whipped out an old- school walky-talky from his pocket and shouted into it:

"Enmity calling. Position compromised. Repeat, position compromised. Begin SuperSucker procedure immediately!"

"Told you we should have tied up his hands, too," Luther interjected.

Before we could respond to that, a loud whirring noise, something that might have come from the world's largest vacuum cleaner, was heard, and everything related to the town- people, buildings, trees, what have you- was being pulled inextricably towards an unknown source. As were we.

"What the hell's going on, Denny?" Sabina shouted over the roar of the suction.

"I don't know. But I got a feeling we're all gonna find out- real soon...."

JOURNAL OF ROB, SECRET AGENT DOG EMERITUS

I was running away. Of course, when I was an active agent, I was always running, away from and towards things. Those days are behind me, though.

We protected the world from really bad stuff effectively, for quite a while, until they somehow managed to find out who we were and what we did. No privacy now with all those high-tech security things going on. Anyhow, some human agencies interfered with us, saying that they outranked us, and they put a temporary end to our operations. A few of us defied the ban and started spying on them in return, and so they found our hometown and moved in on us.

I was running until I ran into Mindy-literally.

She was my frequent partner and very occasional girlfriend back in the old days. We made for an odd couple physically, owing to the fact that I'm somewhat tall on my hind legs, and she's fairly short either way. Also, my fur is white, and hers is a rather fetching (pardon the pun) shade of pink. We hadn't seen each other for a while, but we still knew each other on first sight. We'd been through a lot together, and we were destined to go through more, as it turned out.

Once we recovered from the crash, we talked.

"The Federal Bureau of Investigation's tailing me," she said, adjusting the red bow on her head as she did. "Something about pissing in the water fountain in front of their offices. One, I would never do that, and two, I've never been there, so how would they know I did it? You?"

"Homeland Security," I responded. "Apparently, I took a bite of the leg of the ambassador from Saudi Arabia. Where do they come up with those fairy tales?"

She pulled me forward and hugged me.

"I have missed you so much," she said. "Ever since they busted up the Secret Agent Dog headquarters and threatened to have us all thrown into Guantanamo Bay, and that awful firefight that killed...so...many...of our friends..."

She was crying now, which ruined the moment for me, owing that I'd wanted to be this close to her for a while. Later for that, I guess.

"Let's not talk about it anymore," I said. "This whole thing is going to be something we'll just have to endure. Then, years from now, the historians will be able to call the government on how sick and twisted it's acting right now. Just like with Vietnam, and Watergate..."

"And Iraq," she added, drying her tears and stepping away from me. "Both of 'em. But what matters now, Rob, is that you and I try to get to the bottom of this. Even if we both have to die to get the truth, it's better that not knowing it."

"Well put," I said, stoically.

We could not, however, continue to speak like this. For it was at that moment we heard that awful sucking noise, and saw something that looked like a tornado that had imbibed a whole cocktail of performance enhancing steroids coming towards us...

THE JOURNAL OF PAUL GUTMAN

Jeez! I been sittin' in this airport all afternoon, in what must be the world's longest lineup. How the hell many other people are travelin' in this thing with me? You ask me, this is some sort of crazy mixed-up plan. Anyway, all I can do to stay calm is to write. Good thing the guy in front of me has space enough to spare for a writin' thingy.

Anyway, I was sittin' out on the front porch, drinkin' coffee and writin' stuff down (like this), when Louise, my significant other, comes out, all indignant-like as usual.

"Paul!" she snapped at me, her face nearly as red as her hair. "What are you doing home?"

I looked up from what I had written on the ground and looked at her.

"And exactly where should I be?" I asked her.

"Working!"

"Oh, didn't I tell you? I quit yesterday."

"Uh huh. And you celebrated by going out and getting drunk, didn't you?"

"What makes you think...?"

"Because I can see the imprint of your fat ass in the lawn, is why!"

"I happened to be making snow angels!"

"It's summer, Paul! But that's not important right now. Why would you quit your job when we depend on you...?"

"You know, you could easily get something, if you're so concerned about..."

"Never mind me! I got enough stuff to do around here as it is."

"Then do it and quit botherin'me, alright?"

"Not 'til you tell me what you're..."

"Fine." I held up my hand to silence her. "I happen to be writing my resume"

She laughed contemptuously, as she is prone to do when I try to improve myself.

"What?"

"You know what a resume is, don't you?"

"Yeah. But no wants to read yours."

"What?" I exclaimed. "How do ya know...?"

"In the first place, Paul, most employers don't accept written resumes anymore. Especially ones written in crayon!"

"That whole thing again? Look, a crayon is all I can manage ever since..."

"And second of all, most of the things you're probably thinking of applying for are done by young men. Which you ain't."

"Neither is you," I responded. "Look, Lou. I really think that whole piano bar idea has potential. You said yourself you wanted to get back to playin'..."

"Not like that!"She paused to rub her temples with her index fingers.

"Well, Jelly Roll Morton made a lot of money..."

She slapped me in the face.

"I told you never to compare me to that glorified key polisher!"

"But...he invented jazz!"

"So he said. The only thing he 'invented' was trouble for himself-just like you keep doing for me!"

"Now, let's not start that again..." I remonstrated.

But before we could continue our discussion. a giant cloud of air, like a tornado only bigger, bore down above us. By the looks of it, it'd already taken care of a few neighborhoods, and ours appeared to be next.

"What is that?" Louise exclaimed.

"Darned if I know," I answered.

"So, you didn't..."

"Louise, if I had made something like that, I would be riding it right now? "

"Good point."

We had just enough time to alert everyone else in the house- but not enough time to actually get out of there....

And then I ended up here, for some reason.

THE DIARY OF KAY PLAUSIBLE

Rom and I had just vanquished Doc Draco for what must be the umpteenth time (the guy never learns) and had gotten back to Middlemarch just in time to see the tornado funnels pull up around town. Normally, there was a clear reason- and a clear person-responsible for such a thing in my life, but seeing as we'd just defeated him, it seemed this time that something else was involved. Rom was all set to run off in the other direction in his usual chicken-shit way, praying loudly forsomeone to protect him, when I put a firm hand on his shoulder.

"Don't," I said. "We have to deal here, and this thing won't take care of itself. Not without causing trouble for us before it does."

"Come on, KP!" he protested. "It's gonna come right for us..."

"Let it!"

"Wha......?"

"Look, Rom. Draco's the only guy on the planet that we know of who has the kind of technology to make a tornado cloud that big-that we know of, anyway. However, you and I just went crazy on his equipment, so he shouldn't have been able to create something like this in such a short time with such a small bit of operational technology. Point is, we have to see what this thing is about. That means we stay put and let it deal with us. It's clearly gonna deal with the rest of the town before it gets to us, so if we get picked up by it, too, we'll find out what happened to them."

"I suppose you're right. But what if it....you know...kills us?"

"You've nearly been killed thousands of times- a lot of them by me- and, even though you panicked on the surface quite a bit, you still managed to survive. This is just gonna be another one of those times."

"Well, when you put it like that..."

"Just hold on to my hand, and you'll be safe."

"You're always a life-line for this scared boy, Kay."

"You're not a boy, Rom. You're a man. If you haven't become one already, I'll have to make you into one soon."

"You mean...?"

Before we could pursue that line of questioning any further, the tornado arrived and engulfed us...

FROM THE PERSONAL PAPERS OF ROCKWELL WALLABY

"Rockwell!"

Heflin, again. Not that anybody wouldn't be glad to see their best friend on their doorstep, even if he can be somewhat bloody annoying on some occasions, but, somehow, when he screamed my name into my face so many times, a high number I had lost count of, I knew something was wrong. That was confirmed as soon as he managed to get his hefty bovine body inside.

"What is it, Heflin?" I asked.

"It's coming, man!" he said, picking me up and shaking me like I was some sort of percussion instrument for a few moments, before sitting me back down on the ground and letting me get my bearings.

"What are you talking about?" I said.

"The tornado," he said.

"The tornado?"

"The tornado!"

We repeated this a couple more times before I got sick of it and made hand signals for him to stop. Then, after I had regained my fragile sanity...

"Come on, man!" he said. "Don't tell me you don't know what a tornado is. I mean, they must have things like tornadoes in Australia, too..."

"They do," I affirmed. "Only it's hurricanes there. But why are you so upset about...?"

"I told you- because it's coming!"

"Heflin, we don't live in a state where tornadoes usually..."

"That don't matter right now!" He shook me again and then set me down again. "Didn't you see what's on TV just now?"

"I only just got home..."

"Well, there's a tornado coming towards us, and everyone's going nuts!"

"Like they usually do." I have had too many bad experiences with the folks in this town to think of them as anything other than crazy creeps. (My friends excepted, of course.)

"You got a strange sense of humor, man," Heflin remarked, which is odd considering his is much stranger than mine. Then, suddenly, he grabbed my hand.

"Come on," he said. "We gotta get into the basement."

"Why?"

" 'Cause you have to, man. That's where the weather service always tells ya to go when there's a storm like this. The foundation of a house is always stronger than the other parts during a storm."

"You sure?" I said. "I mean, now that Sparky's down there, I..."

Once again, he pulled me close to him and shook me.

"We haven't got a choice, man," he bellowed.

Under duress, I accompanied him to the basement of my house very quickly. It turned out to be a good thing that I had, owing to the fact that, within a few minutes, the entire place was destroyed, and I was left clinging to a piece of wood that was drifting in the highly powerful wind. I was soon joined by Heflin, who was clinging to a larger piece beside me.

"This is great!" he opined.

"Great?" I snarled back. "How can you say that? My whole bloody house has been wrecked..."

"No worries," he said calmly.

"Again, how can you...?"

"Because we're gonna go to Oz, man! That's where everybody who gets sucked up by a tornado and survives ends up. Once we talk to the Wizard..."

He went on like that all through the trip. However, it wasn't Oz where we ended up...

THE JOURNAL OF RAVEN RECKLESS

I couldn't believe it when it happened. And, honestly, you wouldn't believe some of the stuff I've been through, so I guess we're even there, huh?

I know, I'm not much of a comedian. I'm much more of a take-action type, even though people tend to think the actions I take actually are funny sometimes. But that's beside the point- which I am now getting to.

Plebian Hills, where I lived until recently, is not known as a bastion of tornado activity, which is why it was utterly peculiar to see such a specimen of wind and air poking at us over the horizon and threatening to tear us all limb for limb. Or at least that was my view of the whole thing. And, as far as I knew, there was only one person who could be responsible for this little affair, so I went into the house to find him.

"Tom!" I bellowed, loud enough for him to hear me. My younger brother, who truly has only the same carrot-red shade of hair in common with me, soon made himself known.

"Raven, what are you...?" he began curtly.

"Shut up!" I barked at him, seeing as I wasn't in the mood for his nonsense. I cuffed him by his right earlobe and dragged him into the front yard.

"Were you..." I demanded, pointing at the nearby tornado, "or were you not responsible for that freak of nature over there?"

He looked at the tornado, gulped, and then looked back at me.

"I wasn't," he said.

"Oh, please!" I retorted, cynically. "You easily could have called up PhlegmCo and had them jerry-rig up something to..."

"If I had done that," he retorted archly, "I would only have done it if there was something in it for me, as you know that's who I am. Also, it would have been, as you famously said yourself, 'over my dead body', as you personally separated me from any and all phones in my room after I..."

"Fine," I said. "Forgive me for my short term memory loss. Now, the question is: what are we gonna do about it?"

" 'We'?" he responded.

"Of course, we!"

"Who is the athlete in this family? I certainly didn't earn any praise for my badminton skills... "

"All right." I said. "I'll go warn the town, but you better make sure Mom and Dad get out of this alive, or you won't be alive for long."

"That'll be done- for $5!"

I gasped in horror.

"What?

"Now it's $10."

"Why?"

"Five for getting Mom and Dad out safe, and five not to say anything to Mom about you going potty-mouthed a while back."

He was right. For a fast-living spy, she's pretty tough on bad language from her kids, and by tough, I mean a total beat-down. I had no choice but to accede to his demand.

"We have a deal," I said, gritting my teeth as I pulled a bill out of my pants. "But one of these days, sir, you are going to regret it when all of your bridges in life get burned due to this..."

"Save me the oratory,", he said, pointing to the rapidly closing-in tornado. "We got a job to do."

"Right," I said. "See you soon- I hope."

He went back inside, and I took off down the street, yelling at everyone in earshot to take care and get themselves ready for a huge windstorm. I prayed that they'd take me seriously this time. I'd already run down this street a few times already- once when I was begging my boyfriend to reconsider breaking up with me (he did, the jerk!), a couple of times when my friends threatened to end their friendship with me over some stupid thing they said I did (and I did not), and a few other times when the people PhlegmCo hired as replacements at my request threatened to blackball me and I had to bawl them out to put them back in their place. So I prayed they'd take this call to arms seriously and not think that the crazy little Reckless girl had gone off her meds again. (Not that I'm actually on anything, but I tend to give off the impression that I need it to some people, on account of them thinking I behave strangely. Their red wagon, not mine.)

In any event, I soon discovered that a 13-year old girl, no matter how athletically inclined she is, is no match for a fully operational tornado, especially one that seems quite a bit bigger than the usual size. It all happened so suddenly. One minute I was running in front of it, and then I was lifted off into the air, like a feather blowing in the eye of an extremely strong breeze...

THE JOURNAL OF TEO TOTINO

Well, no use getting upset about the whole thing. I'm in this lineup, and once I get out of it, I'll be taken somewhere. Like they keep telling us.

I only hope it's a good one. And I only hope my pals are like this, too. Hate to have anything happen to them 'cause there the only ones who understand me, and...

Nah, I'm sure they're in here. Must be an alphabetical line or something.

But I don't know exactly how I got here. Better retrace my mental steps...

We were in NoCal Bay, drinking our slush drinks and trying to decide whether we should be going to the mall, the beach or the museum that day, owing to the fact that they are the only real things resembling culture in this town. Carvin was all for the beach, owing that he had just styled his hair and wanted to attract the usual level of female attraction he seems to get for some reason. Lars, on the other hand, was her usual tomboy self, patently wanting her way (again, the beach), blowing her uncombed hair out of her face repeatedly, and threatening to beat us all up again if we went against her. Obviously, Carvin would escape her wrath, but Tess and I might not if we couldn't get our thing together. I leaned into her car and said, "We should just go with it, Tess."I mean, if she doesn't..."

"Hah!" Tess asserted her intellectual superiority to me and the rest of us- not to mention the rest of the kids in our grade- with just that one guttural utterance. "We need to stop placating her like this, Teo. It's not healthy for her psyche. Besides which, I can handle her punching me- or trying to. It's happened before."

"When?" I retorted. "I never saw..."

"It happened in a girls' locker room, a year or two ago," Tess said, adjusting her glasses demurely. Then, with a firm tone of warning, she added: "And that is all you need to know about it!"

"My curiosity about that matter has been permanently curbed," I said, with all the dignity an easily intimidated 12 year old boy can project in front of a superior female peer. "But the fact remains. What are we gonna do about...?"

"Hey!" Lars barked at us. "You two made up your minds yet?" "Put a sock in it, Lars!" Tess said. "We don't have to do everything you want all the time."

"I know that," Lars huffed. "But I have support this time. Carvin just said that he...Carvin!"

Carvin by this time had entered into one of his girl-chasing phases, as one such beautiful specimen had just past him by, and he was running after her.

"Get back here and support me, you idiot!" Lars barked at him, which punctured the spell and got him back.

"Brother can't do nothin' no more," he mumbled under his breath.

"You sayin' something about me, you jerk?" Lars shouted at him.

"No!" he retorted. "I just..."

"I knew it!"

She was going to attack him, 'cause she's like that sometimes, even with friends. Fortunately, Tess and I were able to restrain her before anything bad happened.

"Let go of me!" Lars shouted. "Or I'll..."

"You'll what?" Tess shouted back at her. The added layer of moral superiority in her voice did the trick, and Lars wilted inside her jeans and sweatshirt.

"I...mean...sorry?" Lars struggled for the right words, and for them to come out.

"Good enough for me," I said, wanting to get over this thing.

"Is that all you can say?" Tess suddenly released Lars and turned on me. "After she threatened to kill all of us?"

"I never said I was gonna..." began Lars.

"Shut up!" Tess said, to her. Then, to me: "How can you just stand there and say that?"

"Uh...because you told me to?" I said, my own dander getting up now. "Like always."

"What is that supposed to...?"

"Lord have mercy!" Carvin had interrupted us, with a classic interjection he rarely used lightly, so we knew something was up.

"What's the matter, Carv'?" I said. Then I saw it, and descended into a series of polysyllabic nonsense words, like I usually do when I'm scared. Which is often.

It was a hurricane!

"That's ridiculous!" Tess said, taking a purely objectively scientific view to the whole thing. "It doesn't have the right shape for a hurricane. You can't even see the eye from this angle. It doesn't seem to be natural, anyway. More like someone manufactured it..."

"Dude, forget that scientific stuff!" A suddenly panicky Lars started shaking Tess to get her attention. "It don't matter whether or not it's made or not. What matters is whether or not it kills us! And it's gonna do that if we don't..."

"All right!" Tess broke her grip. Then, to all of us, she pronounced: "To the tree!"

For once, we were in complete agreement as to what we should do. And so we headed up into the branches of our favorite tree, a sprawling oak that'd handled many worse storms- and our combined bulk- for so many years, we were sure it'd protect us again.

We were wrong. The storm tore the tree out of the ground, and despite our best efforts, it threw us to the four winds...

Which is how I ended up here.

FROM THE PERSONAL PAPERS OF BASIL BUNNY

Hiya, 'toon fans! We sure got a lot of—

No, no, no, no, no! Stop it!

Steinberg's gone! He's gone-and he's never coming back! Just abandoned us. So don't go writing like you're still working for him- 'cause you're not!

Now, let's see if you can figure out how can get out of this little mess, huh?

Okay.

Let's see- got up and did my usual routine. Then I went to see Bonnie, hoping that she'd do me the honor of going out with her that evening. Unfortunately, I'd turned up at the wrong time. I might have been mad when Steinberg quit on us, but I got over it. Not Bonnie.

"What?" she demanded.

"Well, uh..." I stammered. (Me and my shyness! She'd be mine for sure if I could be more confident, but...)

"You...uh...wanna go out, huh?" she asked, mocking me as she filled up her chest and sweater with air. "Well, you...uh...got another...uh...think coming!"

"That isn't very nice, Bonnie!" I retorted.

"Well, that's how I was created, Basil!" she snapped back. "I am my own independent minded creature, not some empty minded sex goddess!"

"Is that all you think I want from you?" I finally exploded at her. "After all we've been through, and after all we've done with each other- and for each other? Seriously, Bonnie. I know it's hard for you not having your life filmed every minute, but you gotta get over it. I did."

"Sure.That's because you don't have that much of a multi-faceted personality- like I do!"

I would've done something totally against my nature then- slap her- but she started crying. Usual 'toon bawling, with Niagara Falls down the cheeks and everything, so I stayed away. Until she embraced me in her usual bear hug. "Basil, I'm sorry!" she said. "I'm in one of my moods, and you know I don't mean to..."

"I know," I said. "Just let me go, and all is forgiven."

So she picked me up and threw me onto the grass.

I got up and embraced her.

"What the hell are we gonna do, Bas'?" she said. "I mean, nothing's happened here since the mid-90s, when Steinberg and his crew suddenly decided after all we've done for them that they didn't need us anymore! It's gotten to the point that I'm pretty much a recluse now. Me- Ms. Popularity!"

"Don't remind me," I said. "I only wish that class action suit we filed against the studio had gone to trial, instead of the lawyers getting us those chintzy out-of-court settlements."

"They screwed us there!"

"Well, what could we do? Their money's worthless here, and vice versa. Besides, when we signed the contract, he..."

Suddenly, she broke away from me.

"What is it?" I said.

"Look!" she responded, turning me around.

Suddenly, out of nowhere, a giant tornado was in the sky, bearing down on us.

THE JOURNAL OF HEATHER SNEAD

January 2—-

My family has been through some dumb shit, but you know that already, journal. I chronicled it and your predecessor volumes already.

This, however...

We were kind of expecting the usual regimented family stuff that Dad has always put us through. Have us pack on a moment's notice, out to the airport, and then rush through some sort of insane sight-seeing expedition in a far-away place that usually ends up being connected to his job in some sort of crazy fashion. Mom and I were at home expecting the call any moment, as Dad had already taken Simon and Rodmond ahead with him somewhere. Of course, he didn't say anything about it to us, being that he's the insensitive Stepford Man the CIA insists its people be 24-7. Not a sensitive bone in their body, and that can be said clearly from someone who's spent enough social time with them to know.

That being said, I knew something was up when Mom rushed into my room and told me to come on out of the house. I had conveniently finished packing my bag for the trip (as had she, since she was carrying it with her), so I knew it was time. I also knew, however, that something was up.

"Why so urgent, Mom?" I asked. "You know Dad's usually pretty understanding if..."

"We're not going with him, remember?" she told me, tersely. "This is different. Even the way we're going is different."

I got even more suspicious when she just told me to stand with her on the lawn, even though we easily could have just been waiting for a taxi she just called for. My suspicions were confirmed when I saw a giant tornado peek over the houses of our neighborhood and come down the street right towards us.

I wanted to bolt, but Mom cast a warning glance at me.

"That's how we're going," she said. "It's all your father said to me, so I don't..."

"I get it, Mom," I said. "But a tornado in Virginia? That doesn't make any sense. They're usually a Midwest and Southern thing, 'cause there's more open space there for them to move. And it can't be a hurricane, owing that we're too far inland for..."

"Look, I don't know it happened," she interrupted me. "It could be one of the super-storm things.

"That was a freak event caused by climate change," I answered. "You can't just create something like..."

"The point is," she interrupted me again, "your father expects us to be on that thing, and for it to carry us to wherever it is we're supposed to be. So we'd better..."

"Yes, yes," I interrupted her this time. "Only I don't know how he's going to expect us to be anything other than dead when we arrive there by that!"

Nevertheless, we stood as the tornado passed towards us, and were engulfed by it...

FROM I.M. STONED'S MONTHLY, January 2-—edition.

This month has seen an inordinate amount of tornadoes, hurricanes and other such bizarre wind events across the United States. Something that has utterly puzzled meteorologists while, at the same time, earning the typical knee-jerk condemnation from other nations, who have been typically- and rightly so- assuming that this is simply America being forced to make and lie in its own bed for something they did in the past.

However, there is something else at work here, and, as usual, yours truly is aware of what that is, and is entirely and fully prepared to investigate it.

You probably believe, if you are a regular reader of this publication, that Izzy's simply going to go through his usual routine of blaming all of the right-wing politicians in the U.S. for entering into a secret cabal to wreck all of us. Well, you're only half right. They are responsible for this, but in this particular incident, their victimization extends only to a particular segment of our society and no one else.

I speak here, of course, of the Mucklebackit administration's relentless assault on the animated cartoon characters of television origin, which they have targeted, hatefully and shamefully, for persecution as an enemy group due to a lack of both desire and interest in continuing to wage wars against enemies from other countries. We all know that this persecution has been allocated the funds and attention usually accorded a foreign war, and it has largely been viewed by the administration as such. The fact that these beings are not considered persons in a legal sense, instead being merely corporation-held copyrights, has made this process of erasing them from our collective memories far easier than it should be for the government. We would not tolerate these actions if they occurred to an actual group of legal "people so why are we simply allowing this to happen to these non-people? Simple. Because the government is telling us nothing true about them, and certainly nothing to allow us to sympathize with their plight. These beings are innocent victims of the U.S. government's cupidity and cruelty, and the government's increasingly scary ability to manipulate the increasingly sketchy differences between fact and fiction for their benefit.

Therefore, it is left to me, the one truly sane journalist remaining in this universe, to infiltrate the shamelessness of this unethical operation. I intend to disguise myself as a toon, enter the supposedly secret location of the point of deportation supplied to me by my informants in the government chain of command and go off to Orthicon with the other 'toons. My hope is that my disguise, flimsy as it may be, will still be able to make me a 'toon and that you, the reader, will be able to have a first-hand account of the entire rotten apple straight from the core.

Wish me luck!

CHAPTER THREE

A Commonality of Exile

PERSONAL DIARY OF SAM SNEAD

January 2—-.

Well, we made it. We blasted off not five minutes ago, and we'll be out into space heading towards Orthicon as soon as the gravity of Earth eases up on us. I am now in the cockpit, having finished briefing everyone on board as to why they are here and where we are going. Good thing I have a secret service-style robotic escort around me at all times, care of the government, 'cause I got the feeling when I addressed them that not a few of them wanted to kill me. Some of them are actually capable of doing that, believe me. I've read their files.

Only thing is, I might have alienated myself from my family- not for the first time- when we assembled prior to the launch. It probably won't affect our relations that much- things like this never really do- but a few bad things were said I didn't like and vice versa and it could taint things when we get to Orthicon.

Here's what happened:

I took Simon and Rodmond with me down to Canaveral because they're a couple of big blabbermouths and would have let Frances and Heather know what was really going on before I could stop them. Of course, I had to show them the processing conveyor belt- which was already processing the 'toons when we got there- and one of the old space shuttles from back in the day, which had been refitted and turned into a giant Concorde for our expedition to the stars. Simon, of course, was practically fainting with excitement, while Rodmond didn't seem to give a darn either way, like usual.

Then Frances and Heather arrived via the "tornado" the SuperSuckers had whipped up, and we went to greet them.

"Dad," Heather greeted me, "what is going on here?"

"Can you maybe not say anything critical to him for a while?" Frances asked her. "Please?" She clearly wanted a conflict-free flight, as did I, but Heather's response to that "please" from my wife was clearly no, thank you!

"I already explained that to you," I said. "I told you we were going to Orthicon, and that I was going to serve as ..."

"Not that!" she said. "That!"

She gestured towards the conveyor belt, the 'toons being processed, and the military officials doing the processing. Already, both of the groups were cutting a blue streak linguistically, as the processing methodology was already beginning to break down, and we could hear it from where we were, even though it was behind plate glass.

"Why are you treating them like that?" Heather said. "You're violating their civil rights..."

"Civil rights?" I huffed. "They don't have civil rights."

"Why wouldn't they? They're people, and animals, and...and...things..."

"They were also created artificially..."

"Just like everyone else, you tool!"

"...and artificial creations do not have legal standing under the Constitution. Only the people who own their copyrights can decide what to do with them, and they have gladly agreed to this deportation, as they have no future use in mind for them either as intellectual property on their own terms or as marketing spinoffs..."

"That's just a legal justification for you pursuing a hate crime against them!"

Heather retorted. "You can't expect me to go along with this."

"You have to," I responded firmly.

"Forget that!"

"Well, the rest of us are going, and you'd better..."

"Actually, Sam," Frances spoke up, "I don't know about..."

"What, Frances?"

"We know Heather's just being obstinate..."

"Look at the conveyor belt over there, woman!" Heather gestured towards it. "Is that something to be obstinate about?"

"...and maybe we should wait until..."

"Nothing doing! We only have a short time before the launch, barring unforeseen delays." This time I motioned towards the conveyor belt.

"Yeah, Heather!" Simon interjected. "This means a lot to me, you know?"

"You are not getting away with this, you fascist!" Heather said, ignoring Simon altogether. "I'm going to the nearest Wi-fi hotspot, and I'm going to—"

She didn't finish, because I pulled my gun out of my coat pocket and pointed it at her. I had never before threatened her or any other member of my family like this, but I was running out of time, and I wanted her- and them- to get the message quickly.

"Does anyone," I intoned, "want to die today?"

Nobody said anything.

"Then get on the shuttle," I continued, "and don't say a word about the mission to anybody or anything who might ask until we get to Orthicon. I'll be along as soon as the processing's done. Hopefully, it won't take too long, huh?"

On the last line, I put the gun away and resumed my normal fatherly jocularity and hoped they'd forget the whole thing happened. But I knew Heather wouldn't, from the deadly way she looked at me before Frances took her hand and escorted her out along with the others.

SECRET ORDERS ISSUED TO THE 119th BATTALION, FORT MACDONALD, KANSAS, U.S. MARINE CORPS

Greetings, soldier! You have been chosen for an important mission- to eject the rascally toonies from the green hills of Earth onto the bountiful heaven which is Orthicon, a mere 100,000 light years from our home. You yourself will also get to experience the splendor of Orthicon, however briefly this mission may last, so consider yourself lucky.

Plain and simple, you will be responsible for ensuring, in a neat and orderly fashion, that the cartoon characters are cleared for inclusion in the Orthicon project based on their physical and moral standing, ushering them onto the space shuttle by which you and they will be traveling to Orthicon, and, finally, to assisting them socially, physically and sociologically in developing the terrain for their settlement via terraforming. We expect that this process will take less than a year, barring unforeseen circumstances. During this time, you will serve as an essential provider of normalcy during what is expected to be a chaotic time in a chaotic place. Please remember to keep your temper in check when dealing with these beings, as their manners and morals are largely those of foreigners in comparison with ours. We expect proper discipline to be maintained and executed to the best extent possible- if there are any breaches of this discipline, we will be informed of it, and you will be punished. Don't ask us how we'll know- we will.

Enjoy your trip.

STATEMENT OF COLONEL VICTOR SAWDON [RET.], COMMANDING OFFICER, 119th BATTALION, AT THE TIME OF THE ORTHICON PROJECT

We had, of course, expected that there was to be conflict regarding the completion of the project. No one had any illusions that things would completely go well, given that, first of all, we were working with a large and diverse population of beings, and, secondly, that it was a population that was wondering exactly why it had been...liberated from its homes so suddenly and without explanation. I explained clearly to the soldiers who had been directly assigned to the processing that it was necessary for them to at least attempt a façade of civility in dealing with this group, owing to the above factors, and maintain it for as long as would be possible for them to keep it going.

You can clearly imagine what did happen.

Now, I should be more specific here. There was considerable talk of abuse by the soldiers on the 'toons, and vice versa, but these were absurd exaggerations falsely reported by a media history with a biased agenda towards both the 'toon population of the United States as well as the U.S. military, and therefore must be taken with a grain of salt. However, it was still a difficult and trying process for all involved.

We were specifically assigned to get personal information from each of the 'toons- name, place of origin, etc.- either from the 'toons themselves or through a thorough examination of their persons. At this point, we would issue them an identity card to tell them apart from the others. It seems simple enough, but considering that the majority of 'toons, in my estimation, are natural-born activists, they had no interest in conforming to an interview process rooted in military discipline. We would be met constantly by rude and vulgar remarks during the interview process, or have members of the population run off prior to or during questioning, at which point they would have to be pursued and apprehended. The 'toons have said much about how difficult this process was for them, being treated like criminals, but it was no Sunday picnic for us, either!

Off the record, though, I am glad that someone has gotten around to telling the story of this ridiculous project, because it needs to be told.

THE JOURNAL OF TEO TOTINO

Jan-Feb. 2——.

"Please stand still, sir," the soldier said as he cued up some security device I'd never seen before. "This will only take a minute."

"Sir?" I said, quizzically. "I'm twelve. I'm not sure you should actually be calling me..."

"It's a formality, sir. We call all of the males of your genus 'sir' and all of the females 'ma'am,' as a courtesy and a gesture of respect. I'm sure you understand."

"Genus?" I said, quizzically, again. "Is that supposed to be some kind of joke?"

"Your genus is the one known for telling jokes, sir- not mine."

"Listen, buddy," I said, putting my hands on my hips. "I..."

But before I could say anything, he had taken the thing in his hands and put it between my legs! Then he went over to my butt, and waved it over it. Then he waved another, separate thing over my face and chest, and completed the routine by getting a good, solid grip on my head and pulling a couple of strands of my hair right out of it. After he'd fed the data into something resembling a paper shredder, another machine produced a sheet of paper with some data and my picture on it. He put it into a laminated pass card, and handed it to me. It read:

NAME: TEO TOTINO

AGE: 12

HAIR: BLOND

EYES: BLUE

GENUS: ANIMATED CARTOON CHARACTER

SPECIES: HUMAN BEING (CEL ANIMATED)

GEOGRAPHIC ORIGINATION: CALIFORNIA (FICTIONAL VERSION)

I was going to say something about how I was not fictional, and ask what cel animated meant, but he held up his hand.

"You are to wear that at all times, during the voyage and afterwards," he said. "If for some reason you lose it, a replacement will be made, at your expense. This is because it is our central means of identifying you. Do not ask me anything further about the content of your card, the fate of members of your peer group or others you may know of, the length and duration of the upcoming voyage, or the nature of your future existence or accommodation. All of that information is available only to authorized personnel, and I am not a member of that group. At the proper occasions on takeoff and arrival, the consul will brief the assemblage entirely on these issues. Please proceed to the next step of the processing."

"But I..."

"Look, jerk-face!" he answered, now clearly off-script. "Do you want to make me really mad?"

"Uh......no?"

"Then MOVE!"

I moved.

FROM THE PERSONAL PAPERS OF ROCKWELL WALLABY

January-February 2——.

"We got runners!"

Heflin and I had bolted from the line as soon as we had recovered from the touchdown of the hurricane, in a place which looked like it was somewhere in Florida by my reckoning, and we had regained our consciousness.

As soon as I put two and two together and figured out we were in a kind of assembly line, I nudged Heflin on the shoulder.

"We gotta get out of here," I whispered. "This doesn't look good."

"I'm with you," he whispered back. "But how do we lose the Commissars?"

"Just start running- after me," I said, turning in the opposite direction. "Now!"

That's what we did. I hoped there was a chance that there would be a secret unguarded exit we could sneak out of. No such luck.

They surrounded us, on all sides. There was absolutely no way we could get out of their grasp.

"You goin' somewhere?" one of the men said.

"We don't belong in this concentration camp," I answered defiantly, "and you ain't got any right to keep us..."

"Keep it shut!" the soldier answered, slapping me, dead in the face, as hard as he could. "We own you now!" He would likely have done more damage on me, but for the fact that, first of all, a couple of his colleagues restrained him, and secondly, Heflin acted up, like I knew he would.

"Don't you hurt him!" he said, punching out at the soldier nearest him. "He's my pal..."

"Like we care," was the answer he got.

At this point, Heflin got mad, and reverted to his bull roots by plowing down as many of the guys as he could. Then he hovered over me, protectively, while I held a hand over the eye I had been socked in.

"You better start explaining yourself," Heflin warned them. "About everything! Or else I may have to resort to knocking you down again."

"You tellin' us what to do?" the soldier who threatened me now spoke to Heflin.

"Yes, I am," he said, "and you better..."

The soldier wasn't listening, though. He took his gun, aimed it at Heflin, and fired. To everyone's surprise, the bullet flew through Heflin- and me, since I was behind him- without any damage to either of us. A small hole opened inside each of us where the bullet passed through, and then closed when it was gone. Heflin and I thus felt the bullet go through, but went through no pangs of death or other injury.

However, if we were surprised, the guy who had fired the bullet was absolutely apoplectic.

"Why are you still alive? You and that 'toon magic of yours! I'm gonna rip you to shreds..."

He did no such thing. Two of the soldiers deemed his behavior the result of him cracking up and removed him from the premises. As for Heflin and myself, we were too intimidated by him yelling at us to even think of trying to get away, so at gunpoint, we were escorted back to the lineup.

FROM I.M. STONED'S MONTHLY

February 2——.

I have managed to make my way into the ensemble of exiled 'toons, much to my own surprise. My outfit, as such, consisted of a rather second rate clown suit, with a prominent bulbous red nose, along with a considerable dabbling of whiteface and pancake makeup on my face for coloring. Discovering the lineup, I was simply able to take my place with everyone else, and, in short order, I have managed to make myself part of the gang. Cartoon charactersan be are extremely clannish but can also be quick to make friends. However, should you become their enemy...but, of course, I have no intention of becoming that.

When my turn in the lineup came, I feared exposure, but this did not happen. I was simply asked to state whence I came, since the officer on duty could find no record of me in the files. I simply stated that I had been what had been a vague background character- that is, an extra in 'toon terms, of which the vast majority of them are- on a (non-existent) Saturday morning program from the 1960s. Rather than check my erroneous assertion, however, the officer simply took me at my word, and assigned me a badge with that and additional information I supplied, before hurrying me along.

This troubles me. If the people conducting the operation are so dispassionate about their job that they are willing to accept falsehoods so easily at face value, what does that say about the stability and logistics of the enterprise as a whole?

PERSONAL DIARY OF SAM SNEAD, January 2—-.

As smooth as the takeoff was, my relationship with the 'toons has already gotten off to a rocky start. They haven't taken kindly to our transporting of them off Earth, which puzzles me. And if their reaction to my cleverly prepared address to them is any indication, it's going to take an awful lot to win them over.

As soon as we were out of Earth's orbit, I signaled to the pilot, with whom I was sharing the cockpit, that I was prepared to give my speech.

He obliged me by turning on the system that would allow the 'toons to view me on the hookup based in and around monitors installed in the back of each chair and a large screen at the front, and I began.

"Hello....whatever you are. Welcome to the opening stage of your pleasure trip. My name is Sam Snead, and I am your hijacker for tonight."

Nobody laughed. And I thought these people were supposed to have a sense of humor.

Oh, well...

"Obviously, you can't appreciate a good joke like I thought you could," I responded. "Well, here's the truth. See if you can stomach it. You're being deported from the United States of America..."

Some loud hissing and swearing threatened to drown out the rest of my speech, but our flight attendants soon got things under control by threatening to off the first toon-head who made any more noise, and I was able to continue.

"As I said, you are being deported from the United States of America, but this is, in fact, a glorious opportunity for you to begin your lives anew on a distant planet with a population comprised almost entirely of your own beings. Under the direction of myself as the U.S. consul, we will begin to shape the kind of direction you and you alone want to have for your lives. Shortened and truncated as they may be."

That last line was another attempt at a joke. Again, nobody laughed. That simply got me mad again.

"Okay. You know what? I'm just gonna shut up for right now, 'cause you jerks obviously don't appreciate what we're doing for you. Wait until you get to Orthicon, and then you'll see. You'll be kissing my shoes!

"Look. I'll go over everything in more detail once we land. In the meantime, just sit tight and enjoy the flight. Besides, you don't have much of a choice in this whole thing, do ya?"

My image disappeared from their screens.

PERSONAL DIARY OF MUCK FLECKNOE

Circa Jan.-Feb. 2—-.

"Sit tight and enjoy the flight," he said. As if this was some sort of pleasure cruise.

Boot and I were seated in one of the back rows.. Because he had bad mouthed the soldiers during his processing, they had stuffed a handkerchief in his mouth and applied additional chains and things to him when he was seated. When I admitted to creating him, I was seated next to him, by force, to keep an eye on him. As if he could actually do anything!

I got the treatment the others got, which wasn't better. Leg and hand irons- applied to your hands and legs electronically, immediately after you sat down. They obviously weren't going to let any of us go while we were under their supervision. Not even to go to the bathroom. I don't think there actually were any bathrooms on the ship- since, apparently, the ship was going to go so fast they wouldn't be needed.

Boy, were they wrong.

As soon as the thing left the station, the idiot pilot decided to show off, and he started doing barrel rolls. Barrel rolls- with a space shuttle! Who does that? You can imagine what that triggered in us. Screaming panic to start with, though we couldn't run around in terror to emphasize that fact, obviously. And then those who couldn't "take it" vomited. Total and complete projectile vomiting from a select percentage only, but it still made the air reek. And we were expected to clean up the mess we made once we landed, according to the soldiers. Well, who caused us to make the mess in the first place?

Those indignities I think we could have taken- most of us, anyway- but then Snead came on and made his fatuous little speech about what a great opportunity this whole thing was for us. Please! It was an opportunity for them to practice the domestic terrorism they're so eager to practice themselves but deny that they do it in public. "We didn't cause the [insert minority group here] to revolt- they did it to themselves, and we have to help them fix what caused them to do it to themselves." Yeah, right!

Anyhow, it only took us a few hours to get there, which shocked me. Isn't space travel supposed to take months- or even years- to happen? Orthicon must have been really close to Earth, and nobody must've noticed it until it started serving the purpose the U.S. wanted to have for it.

Namely: to get rid of us.

FROM I.M. STONED'S MONTHLY

March 2——.

Greetings again, readers. I am forced, due to limited circumstances of technological access, to use an old fashioned, manual PC in the so-called library set up here in Orthicon with a strict half-hour use limit, so I will attempt to inform you of my recent travails here in as brief a manner as possible, given current conditions. More on the technology problem below, as I fear the U.S. consular government has made a severe tactical error in limiting and, in some ways, personifying its use.

The major on-flight incident was an attack of projectile vomiting, which was quite clearly the result of the pilot of the spacecraft deciding to do a whole range of terrifying barrel rolls, in which the ship turned at speeds resembling the average carnival tilt-a-whirl- very uncomfortable speeds, at that. If I and the other thousands of guests aboard had not been firmly belted into our seats, along with having chains attached to our arms and legs to further restrict our movement, we would have most certainly been thrown about the cabin of the ship in highly uncomfortable ways, and possibly have been killed in the process. As it was, the vomiting proceeded, largely among those fortunate enough to eat before we got on the ship. However, we were assumed collectively to have caused it, and when the ship landed, we were forced to clean it up at gunpoint, which has largely been how what passes for law and order has been conducted here, contrary to government propaganda (of course).

Once again at gunpoint, we were then forced to exit the ship, in traditional military double-time fashion, since soldiers, typically, know of no other way of doing things except their own. This was how I, and the rest of us, got our first look at the place we may very well be spending the rest of our lives in.

Orthicon is a small planet, roughly the size and shape of one of a larger planet's moons. It is far enough away from the Earth to be considered "alien" in nature, yet it functions in all other respects as Earth's second, largely unknown moon, affected in every respect by this larger planet's cycles of day, night, and movement. However, being out of direct contact with the sun's rays, it is almost entirely barren of the kind of vegetation that would be able to grow on a more heavily fertilized area directly exposed to the sun. The exception is the area in which we are to be concentrated, which has been made to look and feel much like a standard American city, with buildings, sidewalks, etc., laid along standard plans. Unfortunately, it is not entirely a completed process; construction is rampant, and many buildings which likely were intended to be finished some time ago are not. The soldiers accompanying us are seeing to this job, finishing a job left vacant by their predecessors.

As for the native peoples, they seem attentive and eager to please- too eager, I fear, in many instances. It is clear to me that the U.S. government discovered and infiltrated this domain many years ago because it discovered how pliable and malleable the natives are, and soon discovered that it would be quite easy to mold them to their own desires. Thus, in true colonial fashion, this race has been placed to work serving the every need and whim of a race of beings nearly as discriminated against as their own- but in no way are they to be informed of this themselves. Nearly every 'toon in the place has been assigned one of these creatures to serve, essentially, as their (unpaid) valet. Some relations that have developed are cordial- mine with my own, for example- but others have found this much more of a strain. They are clearly not used to being looked after in the all-consuming manner that has been imposed on the Orthiconians, who almost worship the 'toons as if they were reincarnated gods of their planet. This is interesting for a little while, but when it happens for more than a few days...

I am currently receiving angry looks from people around me, so I will now sign off for the time being. Hopefully, I will soon get a chance to speak with you again, if I can book the right time for it here. There's a long line-up...

PERSONAL DIARY OF SAM SNEAD January 2——. (Follows previous entry)

The landing in the terraformed area of Orthicon was a huge to-do. I had been told that they were aware that we were coming, but I didn't expect what we got from them. You might have thought they were expecting Elvis, or the Beatles. The guys who came before me sure did a good job of educating these guys as to who and what they were dealing with!

We were mobbed and nearly overwhelmed as soon as we were able to get out of the ship and onto the land. It was fortunate for us that we had soldiers working on our side on both the ship and the land to hold them back and prevent them from doing anything rash, or else they might have killed us with their kindness.

Rodmond, dressed in his race's ceremonial presentation attire, led me towards a couple of older fellows I presumed were elders. In their language, I was to present myself to them, explain the reasoning behind why the United States of America and Earth had come to colonize the place (if they didn't know or get it already) and then I was to do some sort of hail Caesar thing at the end, clicking my heels. Rodmond had drilled me about all of this- repeatedly- as soon as we had arranged the terms of his being my second-in-command, so I knew my part down cold.

And so I went through the routine with them. I started, and they followed:

It went on and on for several minutes. The Orthiconian language is very dull and repetitive, with some phrases and concepts standing in for a dozen ideas and idioms we have in English. Fortunately, as I explained to them, we were going to conduct business and trade exclusively in English (which, by now, a great many of them had learned to speak from the soldiers who had preceded us) from this point on. That would be a lot easier for them- and me, for that matter. To say nothing of the starving mob I'd brought with me, most of which, I presumed, could barely speak English to begin with!

After Rodmond dismissed them with a ritual salute, he turned to me.

"I think we got off to a good start," he said. "Obviously, the ones who would have remembered me from the old days aren't here anymore, or they would have recognized me. Good. That can help me build up a clean slate."

"What do you mean by 'a good start'?" I asked. "Wasn't that supposed to seal the deal entirely?"

"That," he said, archly, whirling around to face me, "was simply an oral promissory note. We've just agreed to use the land and the people fairly according to the customs of Orthicon. It's not like a treaty or anything like that. We don't own the land and can't tax the people. We're renting the territory from them. Sure, we're running our little spread, no question about that. But they're still the landlords of the whole planet. And if they think we're not doing the territory or the people well, it'll come back to bite us."

I grimaced.

(The diary continues)

...I resolved never to do that again.

In any event, it was time for me to make my first address as consul to the teeming crowds, which, after being rounded up from the holding areas and forced into the seating areas at gunpoint, they were to listen to attentively, as it contained information that would be key to understanding the how and the why of operating in the place. At least, I hoped they would listen attentively. After what happened on the shuttle, I couldn't guarantee that they thought highly enough of me to ensure that. But you gotta try with these things- that's all that counts.

I won't bother putting most of it down here. Getting it down on paper to read was hard enough. It's best that I provide you with just a few salient points.

I told them that, by order of the United States government, they had been expelled from Earth and placed here, on this planet and in this facility, so that they could better serve the country by living the rest of their lives out here. They were simply too different and too strange to ever be considered normal Americans there. Here, they would be relatively normal and free from the prejudices of the outside world, and they would be free to be whatever they were on their own terms. Within reason, of course.

Then I explained that they were going to receive monthly allowances. They actually started cheering- until I clarified that it was to be issued in a special form of scrip that was to only be used within the restrictions of the Orthicon compound. That shut them up, since there won't be too many places on the compound they can use it, other than the store and the cafeteria we've set up for their use.

What really finished things, however, was the fact that we were limiting Internet access to a couple of terminals in our public library. (You know how much it costs to feed a connection from Orthicon to Earth? After paying that much money for that, the Government wasn't gonna pay for wi-fi for this place!) Nobody was to have any other access without my knowledge and understanding of why it was being used, 'cause we couldn't risk any information about what was really going on here to be leaked and found out. (Especially not those untutored jerks who've colonized the Internet with their ill-informed journalism!) Consequently, they were to immediately surrender any devices they had on them which could send and receive signals on the Internet. The older ones who had nothing on them said so, and everything was fine. The younger ones, for whom the stuff is practically a religion, were considerably more resistant, fighting like wildcats when the soldiers began ripping (or trying to rip) their devices out of their hands.

Eventually, the soldiers got the stuff away from them and locked it up in a specially made shed hidden amongst the grounds. Take that, brats!

I closed by saying that I left them to get better acquainted with each other, as it was very, very likely they'd be spending the rest of their lives together, and they wouldn't have much of a chance to meet anyone else, now, would they? Then, with the soldiers protecting me at all angles from any possible means of retaliatory attack (save for the regular rounds of verbal insults I have begun to become accustomed to), I retreated to the safety of the house/office where I was to reside and conduct my business from now on.

JOURNAL OF BRENDAN GUTMAN, CANINE BEING (not DOG) AND PROFESSIONAL (not AMATEUR) WRITER, February 2—-.

Well, this thing is working out perfectly.

It's too bad paper can't express sarcasm. Or anger, or hatred, for that matter. 'Cause I am all of those things right now. I- and about half the universe, it seems-have been abducted from the only homes we've ever known and placed who knows where out of the good graces of the American government. Or should I say, the kingdom of his royal majesty King Samson I!

Again, paper fails me. But it's all I got right now. They keep us away from the computers like babies from rat poison. We can't let our precious babies' minds be infected by that filth on the Internet. Please! They just don't want us to know the truth about this damn thing. But I'm hoping to find it out, sooner or later.

Well, it's not all bad. I met this cute little girl, while we were getting assigned to our dorm rooms, like college students .

For once in my life, it's not a human girl I'm now in love with, but a lucidly-speaking female of my own race.

I was standing around, minding my business, when I heard an innocent-sounding voice say:

"Greetings, fellow carbon-based quadruped."

I turned around, and she was standing beside me, grin plastered all over her face.

She had a big head that seemed too big for the rest of her tiny body. Ears that tapered to triangle points behind her head. A big black nose, enormous blue eyes and eyebrows that let on more than she was telling. A tiny tail that seemed to be wagging her entire tiny, square-chested body. Little brownish dots all over her. Other than a blue collar around her neck, she was naked as the day she was born- which, I assumed, could only have been a couple of weeks ago, at least.

We weren't exactly twins, but we had the white fur and the collar in common. Except mine's red and I haven't got spots. Also, I prefer being bipedal as much as I can manage, whereas she seemed to assume that I was a fellow quad, based on the quote.

"You mean me?" I asked.

"None other."

"Look, kid. I've had a rough flight..."

"I know. I was on the plane, too. Okay?"

The sweetness she had shown initially had been replaced by sauciness. Suddenly, I was intrigued.

"Sorry," she said, being sweet again. "I get moody sometimes..."

"I know what you mean. It's a dog thing."

"More a girl dog thing, but you're right. In any event, I just had to meet you when I saw you."

"How come?"

"Well, when a girl gets a chance to meet her favorite author, she can't possibly pass that chance up, now, can she?"

From out of nowhere, she produced a copy of my novel.

That flabbergasted me. I had been told by my publisher that very few copies of *Love At The Speed Of Sound* had managed to make it outside the borders of my home town. Even online, it hadn't done much.

But maybe that was how she got it.

Had to ask her.

"How did you...?"

"I know. You're surprised. It was a library discard. Apparently, some fool tried to read the thing in the bathtub, and dropped it in there when it was full. What carelessness!"

"Uh-huh."

"That's how I got most of my books. Where I came from, I mean. Those moronic humans have yet to fully appreciate us, Brendan. They deny us access to the library.

I have a library card- I mean, I did where I came from- and they still thought that I meant to wreck the place. They thought I faked the card!"

I realized I didn't know her name, but then she offered her little paw in my larger one.

"I know what you're thinking. I'm psychic, you see. You want to know what my name is, don't you? My name is Cadmium. At your service, sir."

"Huh?" I said. "You want to be my Chihuahua maid, or...?"

She withdrew her paw rapidly and glowered at me fiercely, even making me step back.

"I," she snarled, "am a Dalmatian!" She stood up on her hind legs and pointed to a mark on her face. "Can't you see my spots?"

"Okay," I said. "Sorry. I didn't know."

She took a huge breath in her tiny chest and finally exhaled. "It's all right, Brendan," she said. "Being a puppy in body, but not in spirit, one has to correct those who don't get it sometimes. What's the matter?" she said, severely. "I'm not good enough for your attention?"

"No. I didn't..."

"Oh, I know what it is. The famous author doesn't have time for us. Thinks he's better than the average dog!"

"That's not..."

She got up on her hind legs and started prancing around. "Look at me, everybody!" she shouted, mockingly. "I'm Brendan Gutman! I have no time to associate with common mongrels now that I am a literary success! The people who help me succeed mean nothing to me now!"

"All right, all right," I said. "I give. Now cut that out!"

She stopped and looked at me, grinning.

"Sorry," she said. "Overcompensation for being tiny."

"Obviously. So," I said, changing the subject, "you enjoyed the book?"

"Entirely. I nearly killed myself laughing!"

That was strange to me, because the book was intended as romance, not humor.

THE JOURNAL OF HEATHER SNEAD, February-March 2——.

Well, if anything good has come out of this whole affair, it's that I have started making a bunch of new friends.

The whole living arrangements thing is pretty asinine. We are all segregated- boys in one building, girls in another, funny animals (whatever those are) in another, unclassifiables in one, people working for the fascist machine in one, and so forth. It's a bit like college, except instead of having to live in some second-rate dormitories, we're living in what are essentially hotels, with pools, exercise rooms, vending and ice machines, big comfy beds with umpteen different pillows on 'em, wide screen TV sets, etc. (But no wi-fi, of course, except for that super low-tech deal at the "library"). And we each have one of the aliens serving us in some capacity or another. Pretty creepy...

Anyhow, the girls are mostly from elementary school age to my age, but we've started to bond a bit. There's a few who are a bit more toffee-nosed than the rest, but the vast majority of them are highly accessible. A lot of us have started becoming palsy-walsy, like we've known each other for years. The one I've gotten to know best is Janey Wickman. Get this: she's a robot, and a superhero to boot (or at least, where she came from: that qualifier has to be put in front of all talk about the past from now on). She can bench press more pounds than I imagined could ever exist, and she has a huge cache of weaponry in her body. Look out if you get her mad! But she looks like a normal girl, with pigtails and a blue top and skirt. Subterfuge of the highest kind. Well, her Mom is a genius, sort of, and she apparently couldn't have kids the normal way, so... Too bad Janey's Mom got conscripted into the defense machine Dad's building up to protect us from whatever's out there. We're gonna need more protection from him, given his surly, violent, turn-on-a-dime moods.

In any event, it can only go up from here...

PRIVATE JOURNAL OF STEDMAN G. GUTMAN, EVIL GENIUS (AGED 2 ¾) February 2—-.

I have received, at this moment, a severe amount of pain to my person, of the likes of which I have not experienced for some time. I suppose if I go over the events again, I could possibly figure out exactly what I did to deserve that pain, although, for the life of me, I do not know exactly what it was...

Ah, yes. It's coming back now.

The house was picked up, and everyone was scrambling for cover. Myself, Brendan, the Man and the Woman. I knew not where the others were, but best not to belabor the point.

I remember that asinine questioning session, where they treated me with all the respect they felt was due me- none- and then that ride on the giant ship. Not very pleasant, when you consider that the pilot clearly did not have any of our best interests at heart. Not when you consider a barrel roll the height of sophistication.

Yes. It wasn't until I got brought down to the surface of this silly place. And I now know exactly to whom it can be blamed.

We had all entered the hotel-like establishment reserved for the children. Apparently, whomever designed the outlines of this place presumed to think that all of the groups included under each name were mature enough to live on their own without outside supervision

Undoubtedly, many of us, including myself, are, but there are many upon whom, after observing them in action, I highly doubt "maturity" is a word any of them have even heard of.

In any event, I happened to make the acquaintance of a young blonde girl a couple of years older than myself, although only slightly taller. She was wearing a blue dress with a black line through it. I attempted to engage her in conversation and managed to do so after she turned around to face me. I was enchanted, of course, but who wouldn't be with the likes of her? Her eyes were blue as well, taking up almost half of her face, and her voice and manner extremely innocent., Alas, her two similar-looking sisters, one a redhead with red eyes and dress, the other a brunette with green eyes and dress, took exception to me talking to her as I did. Protectively, they rushed over to us, and before anybody could say anything, the brunette had slugged me and I was lined up square with the floor. Then the brunette rushed over to me with great speed and stood over me.

"If you don't stay away," she growled at me, "I'm gonna upset your backbone, put your kidneys to sleep, do the breakaway on your liver, and dare your heart to beat!"

Owing to the strength of the punch, I was incapacitated and could not defend myself. Neither, it seems, could the blonde. She protested that I did not deserve to be treated in such a fashion, but the redhead loudly silenced her, saying that, as this was a strange place with strange people besides, they were not to speak to anyone until said person had

No matter. If my plans continue to go into action as they have, the redhead and brunette will not know what hit their arrogant posteriors!

The blonde I may save.

CHAPTER FOUR

Phil Ochs Travels to Orthicon and Gets the Back of His Throat Scraped

FROM I.M. STONED'S MONTHLY, March 2——-.

Hello again from Orthicon, friends. Time is short once again, as I am forced to send this message to you under stricter conditions than normal, as I mentioned in the last issue.

So I will attempt to make this as brief as possible.

We-and by we I mean myself and my fellow 'toons- are essentially living as prisoners of war, although the plush accommodations and the obsequious, dim-witted shuckin' and jivin' manner in which the Orthiconians are treating us makes us appear to be regarded in what might be considered a superior way of living. Not the case, citizens.

We require identification at all times to use the facilities, which are limited to what is allowed to us. This consists primarily of access to the library, as well as the store, whose assortment of materials resemble that of the shops in an impoverished city airport (either cheap or expensive, with nothing in between). Other than that, not much to do but enjoy the parks and lakes (very fake, it should be said) or the myriad comforts of our hotel-like domiciles, which most of the lazier among us have shown themselves to be very capable of doing. Those wanting more have found themselves continuing to want- the strain is very visible on their faces. Perhaps the newly opened nightclub, the Steam Powered Dildo, might be able to cure their blues- if they can afford the rather steep scrip cover charge said establishment demands, above high beverage and food prices as well.

Our food supply comes almost exclusively from one cafeteria, which is hopping all hours when it is open, understandably. The fare is very limited- a selection of about five dishes each for breakfast, lunch, and dinner, some alcoholic and non-alcoholic beverages, and that's about it. Surprisingly, the cafeteria, along with the library, has become a political battlefield, with many well informed citizens protesting loudly and often the obvious and disparaging level of gaps in their nourishment and reading material. The consul's attitude: "You will take what is offered for you- and like it!"

Speaking of the consulate: it is quite obvious to me what appealed to Mr. Sam Snead about assuming the consul's job. Few other men in the world would turn down the chance to become a tin-pot dictator if they wished to become one. Mr. Snead flaunts his status and his supposed superiority over the 'toons repeatedly, yet flagrantly ignores any and all attempts to improve the situation or alter the directives he has received and continues to receive from Washington. The man is surely headed for a fall- if someone can even get close enough to him to put a knife in his back, that is. They would have to get past his robotic secret service, along with his Neighborhood Watch style Executive Defense Committee, whose members are often seen enforcing law and punishing crimes of which only Mr. Snead, who pays them lavishly for this purpose, knows the true purpose. I hope the few of you who are still religious out there will pray for us. Never were poor souls more in need of saving than here.

THE JOURNAL OF TEO TOTINO

c. March 2——-.

Well, we've been here for about two or three weeks now- at least, judging by Earth standards of time. I got no idea how they measure time here or even if they do. But anyway, this place isn't bothering me as much as I thought.

Given the fact that we were treated like inmates in a concentration camp on the way here, I figured it'd just be more of the same once we settled in here at Orthicon. On the plane, when I managed to actually get some sleep, I had a nightmare about making boxes or some such thing for the rest of my life.

Nothing could be further from the truth.

The management seems content to let us eat, drink and play ourselves to death. I mean, we all have to die sometime but until that point...

Some bad aspects of this come to mind. The sole cafeteria on the place, which is about the only real place you can get food, has a very-and I mean very- limited selection of food. No vegetarian stuff, which pissed off Tess to no end, but at least the rest of us got spared that indignity.

But not the indignity of no pizza on the menu- how dare they?

And there's only one real social club thing, and it's a night club, except it's strictly 21 and older. Which sucks, considering most of us here are way under that age.

But on the positive side, there's no such thing as school here, which is the ultimate best part. See ya, federally enforced education!

Naturally, Carvin, Lars, Tess and I have come to thrive in such an environment, especially myself. Which comes as a shock to me, considering how limited my social prospects were at home. Most of the guys- even the ones younger or older than me in body or spirit- are nice and approachable, and thanks to the hotel policy of letting us have as much caffeine as we can consume in one sitting, we've had a number of very engaging and enlightening discussions. As for the girls, I think some of the have a fetish for guys with blond hair and blue eyes and/or who are shorter than them, because several of them have, rather boldly, approached me for dates. Who was I to refuse them?

The creepiest bit of the whole affair, though, is that I have to deal with my valet, Rastus, intruding on me at times when I don't want him to. Rastus is an Orthiconian.He speaks English with a strong accent- I think it's probably some sort of New Orleans patois- because he was taught to speak English by an American soldier, like all of them were. He showed up just after I got in my room, and said he was my valet, except he said it like it rhymed with pallet. I had to tell him it was pronounced val-ay. In any event, after he showed me how clothing remarkably resembling my old Earth wardrobe was waiting for me in every drawer and the closet, and how my favorite toiletries were in the bathroom . He said, very bluntly, that he was to respond to my every desire. My every desire. The way he said that word, I clearly got the idea of what he meant, though if this was being said of his own accord or to appease his masters (likely the latter), I wasn't entirely sure. Since he was blunt with me, I decided to be blunt with him.

"Look, Rastus," I said, politely but with a growing hint of frustration. "You don't have to be with me 24-7, okay? I'm not the President or anybody important like that. I can handle myself fairly well for a kid my age. Don't call me- I'll call you if need some help. Get it?"

Apparently not. When I got out of the shower the following morning, there he was, wrapping extremely hot towels around my head and body.

This is going to take some getting used to.

PERSONAL DIARY OF SAM SNEAD

c. February 2——-.

I had hoped for a bigger turnout for the Executive Defense Committee meeting I called yesterday. I mean, there a quite few advantages to the job, as I designed it. You get an extra portion of scrip for the job, for one thing, as well as the...typical...advantages that come to honest people involved in the enforcement of laws in the community. I thought, perhaps, that they would be beating down the door to get in.

I got about a handful of people, two individuals and three married couples, who apparently have some law enforcement or public service experience wherever it is that they originally came from. That'll be good, 'cause they need to enforce some sort of order in this place which, just as a I feared, is beginning to turn into some sort of chaotic thing with a mind of its own.

Why don't I just use the soldiers, you ask? Those idiotic redneck racists would shoot and try to kill any 'toon they saw! We had enough of that kind of stuff on the trip over here, and we certainly don't need any more. They're pretty busy building the buildings that still need to be built, as it is. No, this is different. First of all, the EDC is for localized stuff only. The soldiers only can interfere if anybody leaves the terraformed area, because then we get onto their turf. Their base and stuff is out there, not there. Second, everybody knows people respect the law better if it's their own people doing the enforcing.

So here's who I got:

-A blond haired, lantern jawed guy in a Mountie uniform, who says he was one at one time. Duddy something-or-other, pretty stupidly moralistic surname. Voice like a phonograph record. He sounds loyal and trustworthy, but we'll see about that.

-An toad-like thing dressed up like a British bobby, with the cone hat, the blue coat, and the buttons. Ram something, she said. Not only a cop, but an alien besides. Used to run the traffic beat in a place called Ponchartrain that was nearly all birds, 'cept for her and her kind. She claims her race held Ponchartrain until the birds came in and started killing off her ancestors, which gave her good motivation for verbally and physically punishing them. She's got a loud voice, an imposing manner, and a deadly accuracy with the ol' nightstick. In other words, she's just what I want, and she'll do fine.

-First married couple are a pair who used to do secret agent stuff with an organization called Huron, which was really a front for the CIA so we could operate in the U.S. without the FBI bitching about us poaching their turf. They were a bit surprised to hear that, because they'd always been answering to a computer named Huron they thought was their boss. (Huh.) Mr. and Mrs. J, they said their names were. He's a tall, dark haired guy like me, with a similar taste in suits (I'll have to ask him about his tailor), whereas she is a stone fox with a helmet of red hair. See how they do.

-Second couple: a couple of ghost hunters. Had to admit I found that a little bit hard to take, but they assure me ghosts are as real as "those Arabian guys" we at the CIA have been dealing with for forever and a day, it seems. That brought me over. John and Melody Penton, they said. They revealed that they really have no experience whatsoever in law enforcement, but they have weaponry and know-how. At least Melody does- I wouldn't trust John with a shoeshine, considering how stupid he looks. But if you want one...

-Final couple: a real mismatch. She's a British spy, he's a Knievel type who's American as they come. He's had a few knocks on the head, and it shows it in the way he talks. But anyone willing to walk around in polyester American flag suits all the time is all right with me! Agent L and Rick Reckless are another couple to watch.

I honestly hope this group can do the job I'm paying them to do. After the last few days, with my robot guard and the citizenry increasingly and arrogantly on me about any- and everything going on here, I'm going to need as much protection around here as anyone else, in spades!

JOURNAL OF BRENDAN GUTMAN, March 2——.

Question: When is a library not a library?

Answer: When there's not a book in sight.

Yes, I know there are other things there now-CDs, DVDs, overpriced coffee, stuff like that. But the printed word is the heart and soul of any good library, and its total absence in Orthicon's rather prissily termed *Atheneum* is an affront to anybody who gives a damn about such institutions.

I don't speak simply as a printed author myself. I speak as an outraged American citizen deprived of one of his fundamental rights.

And I wasn't the only one outraged, not by a long shot.

It started when Snead, in his majesty, declared the place open. Cad and I were among the first in the place, hoping to sample the wide bounty of reading materials available for us.

Which was...nothing.

Nothing if you didn't have an imanidiot phone, or Raspberry tablet, or Simpsung palm pilot, or what have you.

'Cause that's all they had- e-books.

Excuse me while I expectorate!

Granted, they had the stuff arranged well enough, though not in Dewey or Library of Congress, like it should be.

But no print books. How could they?

That was exactly what Cad said, with her particular way of speaking putting a particular emphasis on could which I was able to completely agree with.

We sought out Snead and found him amongst a group of our fellow print advocates. (A select group, since the majority of the 'toons- who are wayyyyy too stupid and naïve, if you ask me- seem to prefer using the shiny, pretty stuff.)

They- and the two of us, as well- joined the throng, all of us clamoring loudly to get him to answer us. It was so loud that he had to raise his hands and call for silence in order to do so.

"The library," he told us, gravely, "was structured and staffed according to orders given to me by the government before we departed for Orthicon. We were not to deviate from those orders by any means. Any deviation..."

"Such as actually having some books!" Cad shouted before I stop her.

"Any deviation..." Snead continued, ignoring the interruption, "would have necessarily incurred additional costs that the government was not willing to subsidize."

"So the government cares more about coffee than it does about books?" one red faced, bespectacled girl said. "Is that what you're saying?"

"And it's perfectly willing to subsidize the American electronic publishing industry while letting the print publishing industry go!" another girl said.

"That argument carries no weight," Snead said, annoyed that it was said in the first place. "The majority of American publishers today publish both print and electronic versions of their books."

"Except the ones who can't afford to publish electronic books- or vice versa!" I reminded him.

"And we're making sure that that great American institution, Ahab's, is serving you," Snead continued, gesturing to the coffee bar. "Or would you rather those Canadian communists do that job for you here?"

"We'd rather have actual books!" a voice in the group said.

"Yeah," another said. "Actual books with substance not the junk available here."

"That 'junk', as you put it," Snead responded, "happens to be the kind of thing I enjoy!"

"Ah ha!" Cad said, making herself heard, like a district attorney pouncing on a stray comment by somebody on the stand. "So you admit it!"

"Admit what?" Snead demanded.

"That you've stocked the shelves with the kind of things you enjoy reading and on the medium you prefer, at the expense of anything and everything else!"

"Why don't you save that kind of talk for the girls?

Cad growled back at him and would have leapt at his throat had I not restrained her.

"He's right," a voice in the crowd said. "Plenty of books on the Republicans and right-wing politics, but nothing at all on the Democrats and leftist philosophy."

"No philosophy at all!" another voice said. Then they all began chiming in:

"He has plenty of Bibles, but no Darwin!"

"...classical downloads by the score, but nothing else!"

"All the fiction is by Americans only!"

"No minority groups represented whatsoever!"

"How can he have a library without Mark Twain? Or G.K. Chesterton?"

"What have you got against dogs? All the books about us are meant for children! There are no dog authors at all." (My contribution.)

Snead, at this point, began picking up the electronic devices for some of the patrons and throwing them at us.

"You want a library?" he shouted at us. "This is the only library you're gonna get, so ya better enjoy it!"

The electronic devices hit some people in the faces and bodies, causing their friends to retaliate by throwing devices back at Snead and delight in the fact that they caused injuries to his person. Cad delighted in this, as I thought she would, although I tried to distance myself as much as I could from the growing riot-like scene. Before I could do, Lancet, the bald, bullet-headed, bearded fellow who had been engaged to be librarian, stopped things. Snead made the erroneous statement that we had started things, causing Lancet to make his verdict immediately.

"You are banned!" he intoned severely, as he pointed a dagger-like finger at everyone in his immediately vicinity. "All of you!"

Question: What kind of punishment is that?

Answer: Nothing of the sort.

AUDIO LOG OF JANEY WICKMAN

March 2——.

I hate this place.

Not the people, or the animals or whatever. My friends and my Mom are here, even though they don't seem to have the same time for me as they used to. They have plenty of new acquaintances to get to know and like, the same as I do, so the fact that we usually see each other only at meals (for them, not me, of course) is understandable. As for Mom, she's so occupied with whatever top secret project Snead has commissioned her to do she can't really give me the time of day. Not that we spent too much time together before, but...

What I hate about this place is that my whole purpose as a robot and superhero has been violently removed from me. And I can't do anything about it.

I attempted to do something straight out of Superhero 101- rescuing somebody falling out of a window. Unfortunately, I was stopped before I could do so.

It was by a member of Snead's so-called Executive Defense Committee- i.e. beat cops, and nasty ones at that. If this example could stand for all of them.

She, a creature of unknown origin dressed in a 19th century policeman's uniform, grabbed me and held me briefly. I wrenched my hand free, but she still stood in my path.

"What do you think you're doing?" she shouted at me.

I explained I was doing my duty as a superhero, but she cut me off.

"Your kind doesn't have any legal standing here," she snapped. "Superheroes interfere with the duties of the real police- i.e. me! You try to do any of your flashy union suit business around here, and you'll be busted- straight away! No ifs, ands or buts!"

"That 'flashy union suit' business," I said, indignantly, "does a great deal more positive things than you're willing to admit!"

"For instance?"

"You may think you own these streets, but my beat is the whole world! Do you realize how many times I rescued Earth from peril?"

"I'm not from Earth!" she shot back.

Evidently, I had hit a sore point. For she soon wrote something on a piece of paper and handed it to me.

"A ticket?" I shouted, enraged. "What is this for?"

"Showing me up!" she shouted. "I had plenty of that on my old job, and I'm not having any now!"

"YOU..." I growled.

I attempted to attack her, but she whipped out a long nightstick and smashed me over the head with it before I could do anything. Then she wrote me another ticket.

"What now?" I said.

"Attempted murder," she growled.

"But I didn't..."

"Don't make me write another ticket- for lying! This is why we don't let you have any legal standing. You people are too strong and powerful for us to trust. You think we feel comfortable around people who can kill them at the least provocation?"

"I wasn't trying to..."

"You don't like it, take it up with Snead. I merely enforce the law- I don't question it. Unlike you!"

Then she left me.

It's happened before, but I was never so humiliated in my whole life.

Or more powerless to prevent it from happening.

***

(the audio log continues)

...I had it out with the Suckerpunch Girls and Denny Penton about my encounter with the jerk who ticketed me earlier, in the courtyard. They've become very close to me, seeing as we share a nebulous social and legal status as superheroes here in Orthicon. We all tried to do our usual derring-do at one point or another, and all of us got ticketed by the same rent-a-cop. We decided that we needed to take things up with Snead, so we drew straws, and I lost.

Soon afterwards, I entered the building where Snead's office was and faced his snotty alien underling, Rodmond, who's never left his side since we got here.

"Yeah?"

"I want to see, Mr. Snead," I said politely.

"He doesn't have time."

"He better make some," I responded, without patience.

"Or what?" he challenged. "What can a girl like you do that's so important?"

That hurt. I proceeded to rush over speedily and grab his hand in mine.

"I can bust your skull open, is what!"

He acquiesced to let me in after I let go of his hand.

Snead was working over some sort of paperwork when I entered and sat down in front of his desk. Rather rudely, he didn't even acknowledge my presence in the room until I coughed loudly.

"Ah," he said. "To whom and what do I owe the honor?"

"Janey Wickman," I said. "Also known as AK-47, Global Response Unit."

"Meaning what?"

"I'm a superhero. Me and my peers are feeling somewhat disenfranchised here."

"How, exactly?"

"Well, every time we try to do anything heroic, we get ticketed and told not to do it."

"Do you like getting tickets?"

"No."

"Then don't do it."

"That's not the point!"

"Then what is the point?"

"We are being deprived of our livelihood, and you're doing nothing to stop it."

"I don't see how that's any of my business."

I suppressed an urge to growl loudly and furiously at his obvious cluelessness.

"Look," I tried to tell him. "When I was programmed..."

"Programmed? You weren't born?"

"I'm a robot!"

"Really?"

"Yes!"

"That's funny. You don't look like one."

I let that one pass, even though it revealed an even greater level of stupidity in him than I had earlier imagined.

"Well, I am one, okay?" I continued. "And when I was programmed, I was told that I had to confront and destroy evil, anytime and anywhere. I have enough strength in my body and enough weaponry to do the job...Are you listening to me?"

"Huh?" he said. "Right. Sorry- I just noticed...that...the wallpaper is coming off the wall over beyond..."

"As I was saying, myself and my peers, through no fault of our own, have it as our mission to confront and destroy evil. But we can't do it for a couple of reasons. First of all, there don't appear to be any villains in Orthicon..."

"I thought somebody would notice," he interrupted. "We wanted Orthicon to be a harmonious place, so we specifically excluded all beings with a history of deviant behavior, excessive prison terms, and/or repugnant moral character from the selection process. They're all back on Earth. Where they belong."

"Which is?"

"Surely you've heard of Guantanamo Bay, haven't you?"

I had. But I doubted that even GitMo could hold the baddies me and my pals had fought for long. I didn't say anything about that to him, though.

"Okay," I said. "That answers that part. But the other part of the job is assisting average citizens when they are in distress..."

"Which is the police's job. Or in this case, the Executive Defense Committee's."

"And that's your position on this?"

"It is. They have a particular role in this community, and they are to perform it unmolested."

"What about my 'particular role'? Don't you think beings with superhuman abilities have a place in society?"

"Not here, they don't!"

"What? You racist..."

"Superheroics, as I know of it, is a 'profession' that cuts across race, class, gender, religious and mechanical boundaries. Wouldn't you say so? So you can't go calling me a 'racist.'"

"I can if you hate robots!"

"Nonsense! You've seen my escort guard..."

"They haven't got brains and independence, like me."

"Let me ask you this, Ms. Wickman. Did you have a nice relationship with the police where you came from?"

He had me there.

"Well ...", I waffled, "not exactly..."

"They branded you an outlaw, and tried to have you disassembled, didn't they?"

"How do you know that?"

"We've made it our business to know about all of our...residents...inside and out. That way we can responsibly act to restore the status quo as soon as we can. Even if we have to resort to unusual tactics..."

"...like blackmail. So, in other words, we heroes are unwanted?"

"If you try to act up and do your schtick in public. Otherwise, you're fine."

"You do realize that we are, morally, superior to your cops. We don't work for money, and we'll do whatever's required of us..."

"You're not replacing the EDC, and you're not getting out of your tickets. And that's that."

"But..."

"I rest my case," he said severely.

"Objection, your honor!" I said, continuing his metaphor.

Grasping his tie, I lifted him out of his chair.

"You," I said, "are going to regret this! I am stronger than any of your feeble 'police', and so are my friends. We are going to do whatever it takes to continue our livelihoods, whenever the opportunities allow for it. No amount of lousy tickets is going to prevent us from doing it, whether you like it or not. I'll just leave you with this: one of these days you'll be sorry you made an enemy of me!"

I dropped him back in his chair and walked out.

PERSONAL DIARY OF SAM SNEAD

March 2———.

I have a steady stream of visitors now. People complaining about their accommodations, the food, the library, whatever. Coming in all of the time, preventing me from getting as much of my work done as I would like to. These 'toons are a bunch of total ingrates. . We give them Swiss cheese, and they complain about the holes.

Granted, there are exceptions. Such as the fellow I met with today.

He came into the office with a little piece of paper that he'd crumpled up. He was a little blue fellow, no arms or legs or anything visible on his torso, save for big eyes and a big mouth. Somehow or other, he reminded me of a character in a video game I used to play a long time ago. Didn't tell him that, though. He did most of the talking.

He told me he had an idea for a nightclub, which is something the place really needs. I listened as he told me what he had in mind. Pretty grandiose sounding, but I couldn't be sure until I could look at his drawing.

"Listen, Mr.-uh..." I said.

"Bootylicious J. Krinklebein," he said. "You may call me 'Boot'. Everyone does."

"All right, then, Boot," I continued. "You have any experience running this kind of place?"

"Of course I do!" he responded, hotly. "Otherwise, why would I have come to you?"

"Good point," I said. "May I see the...uh...plans?"

"Certainly."

I looked at what he had in mind. I was awestruck. In a few perfect pen strokes, he'd managed to achieve exactly the kind of recreational facility I had been wanting to have in this place for so long.

"Why....this......this..." I stuttered. I could clearly see that he was nervous that I was going to start tearing his idea to shreds like some restaurant critic with a badly done meal. I put him at ease immediately.

"This is the most original idea for a project I've seen in years!"

"Really?"

"Yes. You have a real flair for design."

"Oh, please! I just wanted to make it acceptable for adult consumption."

"Well, if you're planning to serve liquor..."

"Of course."

"...It'll have to be an adults-only place. If you had approached me with this thing on Earth, I would have put my own money into it. I'll do it anyway! I got enough being stashed away for me when I ever get back to Earth. Why waste it sitting in some sort of bank?"

"So...you're saying 'yes'?"

"What do you think? Come on." I lifted him up on my shoulders as we exited the room. "We just have to sign some forms, requisition some soldiers to build the place, and then it's a done deal. Then we can start having some fun around here. Right, Boot?"

"Right," he said, determinedly. "Fun!"

PERSONAL DIARY OF SAM SNEAD

March 2——. (The following day.)

I was just met by a reception committee. Not the friendly kind.

Somehow or another, they managed to get past both Rodmond and the robot escort guard, whom I have stationed outside the front of the office to protect me from any more unwanted intrusions. That rather intimidating shakedown from that robot girl a couple of days ago feaked me out. This bunch is all girls, too, but the robot wasn't there. That was all right- female 'toons are hard enough to deal with without the added burden of them being robots besides.

There was a bespectacled girl in a blouse and skirt, a carrot-headed tomboy in short hair and jeans, a fiery faced redhead in a yellow shirt and rainbow belt, and a tall kid with red hair as well, which flowed down her back and set off her blue eyes. They looked as though they wanted to dice me to pieces.

"What can I do for you ladies?" I asked, in a tone that tried to be polite.

"You can knock off the condescension, dude," the tomboy said. "We don't need it."

"How was I...?"

"We aren't 'ladies,'" the tomboy continued. "They're rich girls under the control of their parents. We ain't. And if you say otherwise, I'll smack you one!"

She might have done so, anyway, if her bespectacled friend not restrained her.

"We didn't come to make friends with you, Snead," the redhead in the rainbow belt said. "We got issues..."

"So does everyone here, it seems," I interjected.

"...and you're gonna hear us out, you creep!" the redhead in the rainbow belt continued. She might have continued in this line, except that the tall redhead, whom I assumed was the officially elected spokesperson, coughed, and her peer quickly shuffled back.

"You," the tall redhead said accusingly, "are guilty of a number of flawed procedures here. We all know about the library, and your policy on superheroes. So I won't mention the lax condition of the Atheneum, or the policy that has caused my younger brother to become a nervous wreck for fear of arrest. You know those things, and you implemented them. What is not clear is whether or not you approved the MENU choices at the cafeteria!"

"That," I said, matching her tone, "was not set by me. It was set by nutrition experts at the Department of Health, based on the average assumed calorie consumption required for you here in an alien environment on a daily basis. Here. They gave me the book that they used to tabulate the data." I pulled it out and showed it to them.

The tall redhead picked up the book and opened it. She gasped.

"What is it, Jess?" the bespectacled kid asked.

"This book..." she said, disbelievingly, "was published in......1948!"

"Well, no wonder they don't have the stuff we want, then!" the tomboy said.

"Which is...?" I asked.

"There are no vegetarian dishes on the menu," the bespectacled girl said, adjusting her glasses. "Nor are there any dishes for vegans, lactose intolerant people, people intolerant to gluten, or those who are allergic-to peanuts or many other things!"

"So...?" I asked.

"I'm a vegetarian!" the bespectacled girl said.

"I'm allergic to peanuts!" the tomboy said.

"I'm lactose intolerant!" the girl in the rainbow belt said.

"And I'm vegan," the tall redhead concluded. "There are others like us, and you've done nothing to accommodate them!"

"I've practically been starving!" the girl in the rainbow belt shouted. "Here- let me show you how much weight I've lost!" She was going to lift her shirt up to show me, but I and the other girls vetoed that idea.

"So what are you gonna do, Snead?" the tomboy said. "You gonna give us what we want?"

I pretended to think about it for a moment and then said no.

"NO?" they said together.

"No. I do not negotiate under intimidation, nor do I negotiate with hippies!"

"Hippies?" they said together again.

"Of course," I concluded. "What other parents would let their kids eat like that? I'm sorry. You liberal kids are gonna have to live conservatively here- especially with regards to your diets!"

Unexpectedly, the girl in the rainbow belt shouted "I'll kill you!"

She very well might have, had her colleagues not pulled her off me. That was when they made their exit.

ADDRESS BY SAM SNEAD, CONSUL, TO THE CITIZENS OF ORTHICON, VIA CLOSED CIRCUIT TELEVISION BROADCAST, March 2——.

Good evening, fiends!

There! That was...a joke...Huh!

I come to you tonight first to respond to all demands to modification of the living, eating and reading setups for the Orthicon colony. The answer to any and all past and future inquiries is no, no, a thousand times no! What you fail to understand is that I am under orders from Washington not to deviate from my mandate. I am to provide for your nourishment, defense, and entertainment, such as it is, andI am going to do it, whether or not you like it.

Second of all, we are going to extend the powers of the Executive Defense Committee to both immediately arrest and detain those who mouth off to them, which is happening far too often, and also to repress any incipient signs of liberalism which they perceive to exist. I have been alerted by Washington that a neighboring planet in this star system, Bellerophon, is considering a possible invasion of this territory. They, along with other planets here, are no friends of Earth. So consider this action in the terms it was intended to be viewed on: it is being done for your own protection, and no other reason.

On a lighter note, construction has been completed on Orthicon's one and only nightclub, the Steam Powered Dildo, so I invite everyone able to- over the age of 21, of course- to come in and tie one on. I have a need to, that's for sure.

Anyway, this is Consul Snead signing off. And remember: I wish you love, peace, and soul!

FROM I.M. STONED'S MONTHLY

April 2——.

Friends, things have steadily been getting worse here in Orthicon. Complaints are being raised, repeatedly and loudly, about sub-standard elements in the societal structure which the plush façade surrounding us can do nothing. Already, a counterculture is emerging which is openly rebelling against the Biblical pronouncements made regularly by the Snead regime (if it may deservingly be called so.) The recent rebellion in the paper-less library revealed one such facet of who and what constitutes those feeling the heat of hidden, deceptive policies established by Snead and his cronies. Attacks against the cafeteria for its limited menu selection, and vociferous complaints by super-powered individuals claiming that they are being usurped of their jobs and livings by the Executive Defense Committee, have added further fuel to the fire.

However, it is with the building of the Steam Powered Dildo, that magnificent white elephant of a nightclub, and its gala opening a few days ago, that we have now come to see that America's dream of creating a truly utopian colony for its most openly different members has come to a crashing demise. If anything demonstrates that Orthicon is not a liberal's paradise, and that divisions and conflicting ideologies within the 'toon population that no statistician in the Pentagon could have conceived of when this misbegotten enterprise was a-bornin', it is this monumental eyesore.

I was, like most adult residents of the community, invited to the gala opening, and I felt, if only to my duty to you readers to report on any and all aspects related to this community. I had an obligation to attend. But, off the record, I felt I could easily have stayed at home and gotten a more accurate view of things said over morning coffee the following day, so loud, uncomfortable and hair raising was my experience that night.

The building, from the outside, is a garish, pumpkin-like building, painted in orange. Entrance to the establishment is allowed based on two factors. First, one must prove that one is 21 years of age or older. Then, one must be able to afford both the cover charge and the rather steep prices for food and drink. Due to my cautious saving of every single bit of my allotted scrip, I was able to do so, but there were sundry others who were not able to and were turned away, frustrated and angry.

The interior is painted much as the outside is, in the same glaring shades of orange, with little regard or thought put into whether or not this would offend the eye. These interior walls are festooned with as much irrelevant bric-a-brac as will fit upon them, and once again reflect the management's horrific lack of taste.

The proprietor, a Mr. Krinklebein, is a little blue item only about yay tall, who, for the purpose of opening the place, sported glasses studded with what were obviously rhinestones and a (fake) ermine cape draped around his small shoulders. We can obviously see from where this organization derived its fashion sense! In any Earth environment, the tackiness of the atmosphere would become immediately evident to any sane individual, and they would go elsewhere.

Not so here.

Mr. Krinklebein, with a sudden, unexpected streak of good fortune- to say nothing of the obvious, buddy-buddy relationship he has with Mr. Snead, a partner in the venture who spent much of the night in a glorious state of intoxication- has taken not only to ingratiating himself with the little people, but erroneously trying to prove himself their superior.

Little that could be called entertainment was available. No live band, or singers, and precious little space to dance. What music there was came from the good graces of an Orthiconian who has been employed to serve as the DJ. This music was turned up so loud that the volume soon overpowered every attempt at conversation, and the THUMP-A, THUMP-A, THUMP-A, THUMP-A beat at the lower end of the register threatened to knock the building off of its foundation at times. Yet considering that the the place is simply to provide a place for the residents to get as drunk as they can, nobody mentioned this.

At least, not until the one incident that now lingers in my mind as the key event of that evening.

During one of the dance sessions on the floor, one young man carried on so well that his moustache, which was patently a fake, slid off his lips and ended up hitting somebody far in the rear of the place.

That stopped things cold, for, without the mustache in place, the kid was clearly far younger than the legally mandated 21. Enraged at this flagrant violation of the rules, Krinkelbein ordered the music stopped, and confronted the youth.

" What's the idea?" he demanded. "You're a kid!"

"Sure, I'm a kid," the boy said. "So are all the rest of us!"

The remainder of the dancers removed their makeshift disguises. All manner of mustaches and beards were pulled off the faces of the boys. Likewise, the girls removed the glasses and hats they had used to disguise themselves, though they could not disguise the oceans of perfume, lipstick, powder, and paint they had applied liberally to their persons.

"You're not supposed to be here," Krinklebein said. "Sam!"

An inebriated Mr. Snead joined the party.

"You told me we couldn't have any children here," Krinklebein said. "Owing to the liquor laws and stuff. Right?"

"Right," Snead said. "The...laws...."

"We have as much a right to be here as anybody else!" a voice called out.

"No, you don't!" Snead growled. "You gotta go by the laws! One of the laws is: no selling booze to minors!"

"We didn't want booze!" another voice said.

"Even worse," Snead slurred. "Now, all of you, get out of here before I have to plug you full of holes!"

He raised his gun over his head, like a garden-variety bank robber, and fired some bullets into the ceiling to show them he meant business.

The children scattered out of the place, and things then continued on as before.

Yet that whole incident, a flagrant act of discrimination unchecked by any civilized court of law regardless of what the law may be, disgusted me so much that I promptly left the building and returned to my quarters to write this down for you.

Judge for yourself what this means. But, likely, we have come to the same conclusions.

THE JOURNAL OF TEO TOTINO

March 2——.

...We all had to scatter double-quick when Snead started pumping those bullets into the air. Nobody wanted one of those things in them, after all.

I deeply regretted coming there. Of course, Carvin, with his boundless optimism, was the one who insisted, with his considerable charm, that we go and boogie at the Dildo while making that cheap attempt to pass for adults.

"We'll enjoy it," he told me, repeatedly. "Lots of good times to be had."

Yeah, right.

And then, after all that, I got held up. I thought the EDC was gonna put a stop to crime in Orthicon, but they were all there with the rest of the adults, getting stiff, and the rest of us were on our own.

The problem was, my quarters are right past an area which is known as Con's Alley. Con is not a person: it refers to the profession of con artistry, which is evident every day and in every possible manner here in the bountiful land of Orthicon. They try to get your scrip, your American cash if you got any, even personal valuables if they're really desperate. Most of the time I'm well off the streets and in bed when they come out. But not tonight.

The vast majority of the cons are what are impolitely referred to as funny animals. Most of 'em are anything but. Pathetic animals would be more like it. Evidently, all most of these creeps know is self-preservation, shooting, killing, cutting and shaking down unlucky souls.

Such as me.

I was walking down towards the quarters when I felt a gun at my back. I turned around and saw a very young, blue-furred lady bloodhound with a piece in her hands, motioning me to get 'em up, which I did.

"All right," she demanded. "You got any scrip?"

"No," I said, trying to throw her off. "I don't..."

"Don't give me that!" she snapped. "We all get it. Once a week.. Only some of us- such as me- don't have clearance for a credit card!"

Some of us were issued credit cards to use at bank terminals set up around the complex to gain access to our scrip. Some of us were not. Too complicated to explain here, but the point is, I had direct access to my scrip through my card, and she didn't. End of story.

"Listen, uh..." I began.

"Rocket," she said. "If ya wanna know!"

"Rocket, I don't have my credit card on me. I left it back at the..."

"You're lying!"

She was right. Bad habit of mine.

"No matter," she said. "I'll just shoot you, and then what you got is mine."

"Hey, you!" a new voice said. It turned out to be Ram what's her name, the EDC cop who does the vast majority of the footwork for the force. Normally, she's an autocrat in blue, but I was glad to see her this time. She smashed Rocket over the head with her nightstick and threw her back into the bowels of Con's Alley.

Then she came back to me.

"You better get back to your quarters, Citizen," she told me. "Else I'm gonna have to put you in the jug."

"Why?" I said.

"Violating the curfew, you idiot!" she growled, raising her nightstick in preparation to hit me, if necessary. "Now get!"

"Yes, Ma'am!" I said.

And I did.

CHAPTER FIVE

Splitsvilles

FROM I.M. STONED'S MONTHLY

April 2——.

What time has done here on Orthicon! What was a bustling community a few months ago has now become a decrepit, near ghost town.

What is the reason for this? Why, with all the comforts and amenities available to us, should we decide to decamp and leave for parts unknown beyond the central compound?

The reasons for this are many and varied. First of all, the discipline/regulation system has gotten completely out of hand. The EDC, wearing their garish badges of office, roam the streets early and often, catching and attacking in all conceivable ways anyone who remotely violates their sense of decency and decorum.

Then, there is the general lack of satisfaction with the living conditions here, and Snead's hostile and fatuous response to them. He does not recognize them as his fellow humans and other beings, preferring to see them simply as obstacles and detritus on the path towards achieving the kind of ridiculous goals he and the EDC repeatedly cook up for themselves. Krinkelbein, thanks to his fellow Orthiconians' copious thirst for liquor, is about the only one really profiting in any form or fashion from what is left of the American government's investment.

Most of the beings with intelligence, gumption and resourcefulness have now left us to wander around the desert areas that surround the terraformed main compound, so that, perhaps, they may soon return refreshed in mind and body to confront Snead again, if he is willing to budge at all. The manner in which they have departed indicates to what degree the camps have divided. The human boys and girls have decided, rather arbitrarily, to separate on gender lines. Evidently, they have tired of sharing one dormitory with each other, but I do not yet know this for sure. The dogs, meanwhile, have organized their own plans apart from the remainder of the funny animals, due to, again, some imagined but likely possible schism. As I myself am disguised as a funny animal, I will be, forthwith, joining this camp on its exodus into the desert. Hopefully, I will stand the strain of the unknown climate out there.

The camps did not depart without fanfare, though. Each of their dorm rooms had all of its furnishings fully destroyed, its wallpaper torn off, and its bare walls decorated with a wide variety of substances, from water to urine. It was an epic act of vandalism that would have impressed The Who were they still alive to see it. Let's see if Snead and the EDC can clean that up!

PERSONAL DIARIES OF THE SUCKERPUNCH GIRLS

FLOTSAM:

In a way, it was just like the old days. We fly down to city hall, get our instructions, fly out and do it.

Only it wasn't that simple.

We were, the three of us, totally fed up. Not simply because that icky nightclub is promoting epics of public drunkenness and crime at an epic rate, but the fact that, every time we try to do something to correct the problem, those greaseballs at the EDC tell us we're violating one of their laws and throw tickets at us.

Okay, it's mainly that Ram character, seeing as she's the only one actually responsible enough to walk a beat all the time. Because she's totally unreasonable, you can't talk to her and explain what you're doing so she gets it. The cops in Townsberg got what we were doing and thanked us for it. This group- not so much!

So we flew down to the office complex where Snead holds court, smashing through his window and demanding an audience with him. And I mean demanding! The last thing you want to be is in the face of is an angry Suckerpunch girl or three...

BAUBLES:

He didn't even give us a chance to explain ourselves. All he saw was the fact that we had broken the window. "You broke my special window!" was all he said, over and over, to anything we said. Clearly, he was drunk or stoned or whatever: the odor or whatever it was hanging over him was so hard we could really smell it. And that's bad when you can really smell things the way we can.

Anyhow, Flotsam tried to steer the conversation back to what we wanted, which was to get rid of the Dildo. No dice. He not only said he wouldn't do it, but he insisted we pay for his window. We insisted we weren't going to pay for it unless he made an effort to pay for what he was doing to Orthicon. He made a lame attempt at attacking us, which we used as an excuse to beat him up and destroy everything in his office we could get our hands on. We needed something to channel our mounting anger, otherwise we never would have done such a thing. Then we left.

BETTERFIST:

When we got out of the place, we flew out in the desert, in the direction of where most of the kids like us were going to put up stakes. That humiliation at the Dildo was the last straw, man! When we took a breather, I innocently asked Flotsam what we were going to do next. Big mistake.

"Do? Do?" she bellowed in such fierce tones that I stepped way back and Baubles started crying. "How do I know?"

There was a very tense pause. And then:

"Sorry," Flotsam said, crying herself. "But it's been so frustrating, not being able to do anything, and not being able to do it the way you want to."

"I know," I said. "That idiot and his cronies are ruining everything."

"I just want to be home," Baubles said, her eyes full of tears. "That's where we belong. Where we all belong."

We embraced, but I held my head up so they couldn't see I was crying, too.

THE JOURNAL OF BRENDAN GUTMAN

April 2——.

Well, we did it. Cad and I and the rest of the dogs are out in our own camp out in the desert. Our own little Orthicon, if you like. We have committed all of our resources to undermine the Snead regime, at all costs. The other groups- boys, girls and funny animals- are feeling the same way, and we have pledged to assist each other in achieving this singular desire.

We will be employing a propaganda blitz the likes you've never seen. Tracts, pamphlets, leaflets, internet videos, what have you. Cad naturally has taken a leadership role, alongside Rob and Mindy, the two secret agent types we befriended back in town. I myself am content more to just do whatever they tell me to do. My own attempts at social organization have been failures, as you know, and I, in no way, want this to happen here. But if any of our videos goes viral, look out, world.

I'll let you know if anything comes up. Nothing yet.

THE JOURNAL OF HEATHER SNEAD

April 2——.

We girls have organized ourselves to accomplish our goals, which is more than can be said for many of those lazy-ass boys down the road from us. The less said, the better...

Despite my handicap of being related to my father, I was elected President, so I will assume the main leadership duties of our enterprise. I will redeem the Snead name, whatever the cost! Joining me in leadership will be Jess Penton as vice-president, who says she's going to use this opportunity to pursue work on that thesis of hers she's always planning; Inga Thrid, she with the black hair, black boots, black dress and white skin, as secretary, appropriate considering her photographic memory; and Raven Reckless, who will serve as the executive producer of our media projects. The Suckerpunch Girls and Janey Wickman have volunteered to alternate as the camp's sergeants-in-arms and also to perform reconnaissance missions back to Orthicon when we need new information.

Although we're living apart from the boys, we will be working in conjunction with them on the media projects, at least the more resourceful and enterprising ones. A couple of them, Mr. Flynn and Mr. Fletcher, were kind enough to build us a nice shack out of nowhere to serve as our base of operations, while ace mechanic Shelby Lint and his colleagues are busy working on means to defend us should our perimeters be violated in any way. All the way, busy, busy, busy out here.

I think the environment we have out here- working together for a common goal- makes life much better for us than it was in stuffy old Orthicon. I just hope it can stay that way.

THE JOURNAL OF BASIL BUNNY

April 2——.

Man, that trashing of the hotel room was the most fun I've had in years! Too bad we could only do ours, but everyone else did the numbers on theirs, besides.

Bonnie's gotten livelier, as well. I haven't seen her this happy in ages. But what would make us even happier would be if we go home, forever.

Still, we gotta make do with what we have. We're out with the funny animals now, in the desert, prepping for whatever it is we're gonna do in the war against Snead. At least among our kind we get some respect. Even the dogs treated us badly in Orthicon- and they weren't so high and mighty to begin with!

But we'll show Snead what we're made of, and very soon. We do not allow insults and humiliations to deter us, ever. And that jerk has done plenty of both!

THE DIARY OF FRANCES SNEAD

April 2——.

I finally had the talk I needed to have with Sam.

It's not like it was at home here on Orthicon. First of all, Heather and Simon were off living in the dormitory by themselves, and then they went off to that desert area, where who knows what will happen to them? Even Rodmond doesn't live here in the consular palace so, even though he can be a real jerk sometimes, I don't even have his company to console me.

And Sam: well, he claims to be working like crazy (which I doubt) in the comfort of his office most of the day and then spends hours more at the night with that little blue schmuck at the Dildo, watching all the dumb rubes (who are about the only people left in the main compound now, everyone else having gone) bump and grind and pay highly expensive prices for booze they could get on the cheap back in the U.S.

So we just didn't have the time, and I don't have the company, to vent about how bad I feel, except to you. Yes, there is the small army of Orthiconian servants around us all the time, but they don't count.

Most of them don't seem to have the brains to understand what is going on here- on their own planet!.

It's enough to make me wish I was back like it was before I met Sam, back when I was a groupie. At least I got something out of it, then.

No, you can only take so much, and then attention must be paid!

That's what I finally did when Sam got back. I made my stand. Fortunately, he wasn't drunk, for once, so I hoped this was a good time to talk.

It wasn't.

"Sam," I said, "we need to talk."

"About what?" he said.

"Everything here."

"What is the matter with you, Frances? Don't you have everything you ever wanted?"

"No, I don't."

"Look, I got enough of that 'you're totally wrong and you need to do things differently' crap from the residents. Don't you start joining in with them."

"Maybe I should. They have a point."

He was upset by that remark, as I hoped he would be.

"What is that supposed to mean?" he said.

"You're a dictator."

"That's rather harsh. I'm just doing my job, like I'm supposed to..."

"You don't have to do everything by the letter on every occasion. That's what you always do. You only follow the orders or suggestions of anyone you think is important. Everyone else who doesn't think the same as you can forget it. Including me."

"Oh, come on," he said. "My following orders from the Pentagon is not at all the same as you asking me to take out the garbage..."

"You never did that at home, anyway."

"Because I was working. You know my hours."

"Yeah, I know your hours. But now, your hours are all about being with Rodmond and Krinkelbein than me."

"First of all, Rodmond is my executive secretary and liaison with the Orthiconians, so I have to be with him a lot of the time. Second of all, Boot is a very... excitable... being... with a flair for showmanship, but he doesn't know a thing about business. I have to help him out with the accounts and the suppliers. Booze doesn't come cheap, you know. And we're going through it faster than Congress can increase the size of the national debt! "

"In other words, he's your front. He gets to party, and you get to profit."

"That's a crude way of putting it, but...yes."

"Sam, I can't deal with this anymore. I need to get out."

"Then get out. A walk will do you some good."

"Not like that, you idiot!"

A sudden, horrific realization came to his eyes.

"Oh, no!" he exclaimed. "No! Frances, you wouldn't! After all we've been together..."

"There isn't anything else between us, Sam. I know that now. I realized that before the kids became teenagers, but I kept it together so you would look good. All the drinking and carousing and everything you seemed to be capable of then, I could forgive. You bringing Rodmond into the household without telling me after he got banished from this place, I could forgive. But not the way you've been acting recently. Paranoid and unhinged. I don't like this Sam Snead, and I don't think I can live with him anymore."

"Then don't!" he said, petulantly. "You can go live in one of the dormitories. We've got a surplus of vacancies there, now."

"Whose fault is that?" I asked.

"Just remember, Frances," he warned me, as I left the house with only my purse and the clothes on my back with me. "We're stuck here until I finish my term. I don't know when I'll be relieved. But, until then, even if we don't share a bed, we'll still have to share a planet."

He walked out in one direction, and I walked out in another.

PERSONAL DIARY OF SAM SNEAD

April 2——.

My life has hit rock bottom. Frances walked out on me.

She was too good for me. I'm surprised she stuck around as long as she did. We had some good years, including a couple of kids who are also not talking to me, but everything comes to an end, eventually. I only just realized that.

I have Rodmond, and Boot, and the EDC, all loyal and willing to serve me. But they can't give me the kinds of things I used to have with Frances.

Actually, it wasn't that so much as it was the meeting we had about tonight about Bellerophon. But Frances walked out on me after that, so it kind of put a capper on a bad day for me.

I gathered the EDC, along with our two staff scientists, Professor Euphonium and Doctor Wickman, to talk about what we could do about the whole thing. We were just about to enjoy a rare alcohol free bull session (neither the Prof nor the Doc drinks alcohol, so we accommodated them), when the new bane- among many- of my existence dropped around, and he, indeed, was drunk.

His name is Paul Gutman.

The guy is a fat freeloader who never shuts his yap. He always seems to have some stupid idea going on about how to improve things around here. Not like Boot; Boot's a genius! The Dildo makes money hand over fist, and he's in his element boogieing on the floor with me and everyone else to the tunes. But Gutman...he's stupid , never gives up and never gives a damn besides, which is what makes him so difficult to deal with.

Anyhow, he shows up in the basement grotto where I have my meetings now. We couldn't have it in my office after those loudmouthed bullies the Suckerpunch Girls trashed it. (Turns out they're the Prof's kids, but he assures me he didn't tell them to do it, or anything like that. Phew!) Anyhow, the grotto holds more people, and it has more of a casual flair. Which is what I want to be more of now. Casual. Try to get rid of this thing Frances said about me being a dictator. Then maybe she'll come back...

Where was I, now? Right. Gutman.

The fat guy was completely looped, but he thought he could contribute something to the progress of our meeting.

"Hey guys," he drawled, in that irritating New England brogue of his. "Whatcha doing?"

I walked over to him and, politely, whispered to him: "Get out of here."

"Or what?" he challenged me. "You gonna make me leave this place? Like everyone else? Like you made my kids? And my dog? There's nobody left I'm related to here, 'cept my wife. And she ain't been no fun, as of late."

He had hit a sore point, but I tried to disguise it in my tone of voice.

"You weren't invited to this affair, Gutman. You have no part in. So it's best that you leave."

" Oh, I gotta leave, huh? Why don't you leave?"

"What?"

"I said..."

"I heard you! But I can assure you I have no need nor desire to leave. You, on the other hand..."

For a drunk man, he moved very quickly, and had soon smashed his empty beer bottle over my head, knocking me out.

When I came to, the crowd surrounded me, along with Gutman's wife, Louise, who had been in pursuit of him. She had sent him home to bed before I regained consciousness.

"I'm sorry that you had deal with that," she told me. "Things have been so bad around here recently that he's been drinking even more than usual. He's really changed since we got here."

"He's not the only one," I said, ruefully.

Chapter Six

The Plots Thicken

JOURNAL OF PROFESSOR JAMES EUPHONIUM

April 2—-.

I have been working on what I can basically describe as...nothing.

My conscription into the Defense department, such as it is, was very much like my arrival in Orthicon: unwanted and undesired. There seems to be nothing to do here, and nothing to do it with. Consul Snead blithely assumes that we will could be attacked at any moment and wants us to be prepared for that eventuality. But with what will we prepare? There are no natural resources on this planet, and no way of building anything in the way of defense. Now that the Army troops have gone back to Earth, that's become even more of a concern.

Doctor Wickman, my fellow scientific conscript, and I have resorted simply to elaborate ruses to reassure Snead that we are, in fact, trying to mine some scientific wealth out of this barren land. But most of the time, we're just drinking coffee and complaining about all the aggravation our super-powered daughters have caused us. At least we have that, aside from the science background, in common. Otherwise, I find her hard to approach. Typical for me.

Speaking of my daughters, though: I finally got to see them again today, after what seems like a dog's age.

They happened to notice me when I was walking home and flew down to see me. The reunion was, of course, joyous, even if it was very brief.

We exchanged information. Nothing much had really happened to me, and I told them that. They, however, had been through the mill, and I did my best to comfort them.

You cannot imagine how it feels to see your creations- almost your own flesh and blood- systematically denied what it is their destiny to have and achieve. I tried to design them to be perfect little girls, and while they aren't that entirely, they came as close to that for me as you can imagine. They were meant to keep evil and injustice at bay, and they had few peers at doing that. Now, however, the Snead regime has prevented them from doing that. Only his police and no one else are allowed to deal with crime, no exceptions, regardless of how dangerous or difficult the work might be. They had words about it with Snead, and they wrecked his office and him when he wouldn't be responsible. So they obviously couldn't stay, even though I wanted them to. They're working with their new friends to help topple Snead's regime, and, for such a thing, I cannot deny them that. I never could.

They soon had to leave, and I was hustled off the streets by the curfew imposed by virtue of Snead and his goons. But he clearly does not know- yet- how much of a fall he is headed towards...

FROM I.M. STONED'S MONTHLY

May 2——.

I am now officially embedded with the funny animals in their encampment east of the main Orthicon compound. This is part of the strategy the rebel groups agreed upon when they left the comforts of the terraformed area of the planet. The dogs are living in the extreme western quadrant nearest the terraformed community, the largely erroneously named children are in the north, and, as noted, the funny animals here are in the east. The idea being, when and if the call is given to attack the terraformed area, Snead's comically inept Executive Defense Committee will be surrounded on three sides and be able to do absolutely nothing to stop an invasion. A rather clever strategy, at that.

I now wish to explore with you the experience of two of these beings, whom I have befriended, so that you may be better aware of the great toll this experience is taking on all involved.

Basil and Bonnie Bunny (no relation) were leading characters in a television program dating from the 1990s who were among the first wave of exiles to be expelled from their native land. Their careers, as had those many of their peers, had gone into permanent limbo following a falling-out with their one-time patron, Mr. Steinberg, and a bitter lawsuit that they filed against him to recoup monies he felt that they owed him for their services. They were paid working people's wages by Steinberg's studio for what essentially was a documentary study of life in their native land, while he promptly made millions by selling them for exhibition on television.

Sadly, this is a common practice. The filming of the lives of so-called 'toonies occurs regularly without their knowing it, and they were cruelly exploited in this fashion long before their detention on Orthicon, it seems. Basil and Bonnie claim their ancestry extends back to forebears working in the early days of cinema, whose ancestry, in turn, could be extended all the way back to the Faerie kingdom of the ancient British Isles. If they can be believed. And certainly compared to Sam Snead and all who sail in him, they can.

Our relationship began almost immediately after we arrived in Orthicon. They were, unlike the soldiers conducting the processing, able to see through my disguise immediately, and they further recognized my face: they are subscribers to the "Monthly", and are familiar, as you are, with the silhouette of my head gracing the title page. I encouraged them to keep my secret, and they agreed. Only you, therefore, know the truth, as always.

They were quick to dismiss the stereotypes projected upon them, even by their fellow Orthiconians, as falsehoods.

"Those human beings are out for themselves, Stony," Basil told me. "If we didn't have hating Snead in common with 'em, we wouldn't have any real truck with 'em. Neither would the dogs- also out for themselves, if you get my drift. But the humans are the worst. All this time they've been trying to pass, and now they're gonna find out they can't, and it'll kill 'em inside to find out the truth."

"Pass?" I asked.

"Pass!" Bonnie added. "You know- like you were doing!"

" Ah," I said.

"But it's not a conscious form of passing," she continued. "They don't know that they're not real human beings. All they knew was the world they lived in, like Basil and I did. Now that those worlds have been taken away from all of us, and we have to figure out how we're gonna live together from now on."

"It's not gonna be easy," Basil concluded. "Seriously. When you've gone through what we've all gone through, getting yourself together again, and trying to work with people who've gone through things as bad as you, or worse, is gonna be even harder than rebuilding Humpty Dumpty."

Amen.

FROM "THE NEW YORK TIMES"

May 5, 2——

WASHINGTON (AP)- Another in the round of protest against the forced exile of animated cartoon characters on the planet Orthicon occurred today, this one in the seat of federal power. Yet, rather than be shamed or intimidated by the actions, the government chose to commit the cowardly act of shooting and killing the practitioners on sight.

The tragedy of this action, however, comes not simply in this action alone, bad enough as it is. It is that the victims were all children and young adults, with lives ahead of them fully cut off by police brutality.

The Orthicon project, launched in January, was originally performed and executed under a canopy of secrecy, as is commonplace among government espionage projects. However, the truth began leaking out about the project a month ago, in part due to the heroic efforts of journalist I.M. Stoned, reporting from the heart of the planet for readers of his monthly journal. We have since become very well acquainted with the how and why of this project, including the vicious political bias with which it was conceived and carried out, as well as the population who was its target.

The sudden and irrevocable withdrawal of animated programming from television, however, was what pushed things to the boiling point. Say what you want about the children and youth of America: they will not put with the sudden absence of a thing they have come to depend on for entertainment for much of their lives. Peaceful demonstrations have in the last month multiplied across every community in the country, with one aim: bring the 'toons home and get them back on the air, stat.

Most of these protests went off with little incident. What happened in Washington was the exception, but it is a gravely excessive exception nonetheless.

It is not known who gave the order to fire actual bullets at the protesting children, but once it was given it could not be undone. Nor can the five lives lost to machine gun fire be fully restored to us, to our lasting shame.

THE JOURNAL OF HEATHER SNEAD

April 2——.

"We all saw what happened in Washington, right?" Heather said.

"Yeah."

"And we all think it was bad, right?"

"Right."

"Good. We're on the same page, for once."

One of the benefits of leaving the U.S. government compound was that we all got our computers and phones back after Dad confiscated them. He had them all put inside a little building with a door like one on an old-fashioned outhouse, which shows you what he thinks of modern electronic technology. We made sure to raid it once we found out where it was, just before we left the place for good. Everyone got their stuff back; most of them were kind enough, like me, to label them with their names before they got stolen. And so we saw the kids in Washington being offed, because they wanted the cartoon characters- i.e. us- back home in the U.S. Which is where we've wanted to be all along.

As soon as we could, I called a joint meeting of my staff with members of the other two groups. For once, we'd been able to put aside the differences that had become visible and virulent between us ever since Orthicon began. Dad had systematically played us off against each other, and systematically denied us our worth and dignity with his high-handed, asinine treatment of us. Now, we were planning to get our own back.

"So we're agreed, then," I concluded, after a bit more procedural back-and-forth. "We have to exploit the popularity loophole now, before the scumbags that employed so many of us find a way of discrediting us in the public eye and turn the masses against us. So we have to act, and act fast. We all ready to do that?"

"Yeah!" said everybody else in the room, proudly and defiantly.

PERSONAL DIARY OF SAM SNEAD

April 2——

Nearly everyone gone, now.

Sent the EDC off on patrol. See if they can find any of those brats 'n' dogs 'n' stuff and beat them for what they did while they were here, and for running away like cowardly little twerps...

Boot's here with me. Had to shut down the Dildo 'cause only drunks coming there now. So he and I are camping out here with all the booze and goin' through it 'fore it rots. Got that crap Orthicon music out of there, and brought my personal jukebox from my office. Put on some tasty soft-rock to soothe my nerves. The two of us, we got nothing to live for. They're gonna come for us soon, all of 'em, and kick our asses, for whatever it is they think we did to them.

It's all Bollock's fault. "Don't give 'em an inch, 'cause they'll take a mile," he said.

Jeez! He knew that the were willing to push us back when we pushed them!

Too late to turn back now.

FROM "THE WORLD AT SIX", CBC RADIO

May 2—-.

...The government denied today that it has any plans to exile Canada's so-called animated cartoon characters into space, after the fashion of the highly publicized American Orthicon debacle. The Prime Minister has insisted that this notion has come about solely because he has a friendly relationship with President Mucklebackit, and that it is entirely a pipe dream. However, the Liberals and NDP both vigorously attacked the government's attitude, in particular its television campaign against the presence of these evil beings on the Canadian airwaves, and further allege that the government has been funneling large amounts of money to the Orthicon cause under the guise of payments to American businesses friendly to Canadian business interests in the U.S . They maintain that they will not cease attacking the government until it revokes its support for the Orthicon project fully and entirely.

Meanwhile, President Saunders Mucklebackit has continued his campaign against the press. The most recent and blatant example of this has been his frequent practice of releasing vicious attack dogs against reporters who ask questions he does not want to answer...

CHAPTER SEVEN

Help From Unexpected Sources

THE JOURNAL OF BRENDAN GUTMAN

June 2——-.

Well, it's official. Cad and I are done now- according to her. Our love just fizzled out like a Roman candle, and I can't figure out what happened.

Maybe if I'd just kept my mouth shut...

She came into the tent we were sharing in a rage, nearly shredding the outside flap.

"I have had it with this whole misbegotten 'alliance' between unsupportive, unsympathetic human beings, idiotic 'funny animals', dimwitted dogs, and us!" she said.

"What'd they do now?" I said. Our meager resources being unable to provide for the publicity blitz we wanted, we had teamed up with the other anti-Snead groups to make our forces were properly united. Unfortunately, we dogs had been undercut in the process. We had no members on the governing board, little voting power, and the board had to approve whether or not our plans were a worthy expenditure or not. I've been feigning indifference, since I'm pretty used to this sort of thing, but most of the other dogs were furious about being left out.

So was Cad. But given that she's pretty smart, it only hurt her more, and she was taking it out on me, since I was her only outlet.

"They know absolutely nothing about presenting a message," she said.

"Was it a good idea?" I asked, to get her off that topic.

"Of course it was a good idea, muttonhead!" she responded. "Look at it!"

She handed me a piece of paper.

On it was written this:

A WHOLESALE MASSACRE OF THE INNOCENT

was planned, but cancelled, so we tried to stage

A RITUALIZED DISPLAY OF RUTHLESS BLUNT FORCE

but nobody wanted to volunteer for it, so instead we thought about

FIREWORKS

but we didn't have any, so instead we said that we would do

A CIVIL RIGHTS RALLY

only nobody here knows what civil rights are anymore, so we called it a

PICNIC

instead. So that's what it is.

A PICNIC

THE TROUBLE BEGINS AS SOON AS WE CAN GET IT TOGETHER!

"And they didn't like it?" I said, when I finished reading.

"No," she drawled. "They did not! They liked the idea of the public picnic, but. otherwise, they decided to take nothing from my idea! They said it was too deceptive a practice. They said somebody might think I was being too serious about that 'massacre'. I responded that many famous authors had circulated similar leaflets fort their lecture tours. And somebody had the colossal gall to say they had never heard anything about that!"

"Scandalous!"

"So, I decided we dogs should secede from the alliance and form our own group."

"What would it be like?"

"The Black Panthers."

And she slapped a little black motorcycle cap on her head.

"Oh, no!" I said.

"What's the matter with that?"

"Well, you know..."

"I think it was rather enterprising of them to accomplish what they did, don't you think?"

"Oh, yes. Emulating a tribe of criminals and rapists is exactly what we need to be doing right now, don't you think?"

She evidently was displeased by my sarcastic response, for her face turned incredibly sour.

"We are done, Brendan!"

"Wait....What?"

"I will not stay any longer with someone who ridicules my dreams and desires! You are in league with those fools! I only saw that recently, the way you let those humans make us give up power."

"C'mon, Cad! I'm just so used to humans giving me orders that I just..."

"Well, I am not! And they will see how not used to I am soon enough!"

"Listen. Can't we just..."

"You had your chance!" she growled at me, before turning and walking away.

Girls are funny sometimes.

But now I'm sad.

THE PRIVATE PAPERS OF MR. WILLIAM LANCET

June 2—-.

Snead called me this morning, telling me his next idea for the library.

"I would prefer not to," I told him, as always, and hung up.

Then I informed Professor Euphonium and Doctor Wickman, who have taken refuge in the library after Snead crawled into the Dildo, as well as Mrs. Snead- or, I should probably now say, Frances- who joined us in here after leaving him. We are all aware of the growing levels of unrest in the outside regions, and we have reasoned that we will be safer in here than elsewhere until it resolves itself. We have food and drink from the coffee shop, as well as access to the cafeteria through the skywalk overlooking the road between the two buildings. The fact that most of the buildings are connected through the skywalks allows us to avoid going outside as much as possible, which is about the only consolation we have.

We only wish we could do more to stop things ourselves. We are beings used to asserting authority- they as parents, I in my old job as a high school teacher, which seems like such a lifetime ago. That we can do nothing to stop this bothers us all completely, the others even more so because they have children involved as combatants in this affair.

Yet circumstances dictate that we must be spectators, and that is what we will remain.

I only hope that both sides will realize they were in the wrong and find some settlement soon. For, as my old friend Shakespeare said, the fault lies not in our stars, but in ourselves.

THE JOURNAL OF HEATHER SNEAD

June 2——.

I have been usurped! Or so it seems. The fragile alliances between us have already grown thin, for lack of a firm leader to help us shape our destiny. I assumed I would take this role. But it was not to be. For she arrived.

We girls had gathered for a bull session, trying to find some way of doing something to Snead that all of us, not just we girls, could agree on. It wasn't working. Too much estrogen, too little sleep and our enormously competitive egos were all working against us.

That was when, with her customary precision timing, Leslie Stinson walked among us.

Yes! That Leslie Stinson!

Who hasn't heard of The Stinsons? That show has been on the air so long it isn't even funny anymore. Really. But that was a TV show, and she was a fictional character...

Yet here she was, in the flesh, in her red dress and shoes, her pearls, her pointed head.

What was going on?

Before I knew it, everybody except me was bowing and scraping in front of her. Literally! We all knew the incredible things she did, the powerful people she'd disarmed with her deceptive appearance, her cunning intelligence and her jackhammer tongue. But only I remembered she supposedly wasn't real and kept my place.

Raven Reckless was the worst bootlicker of all. She was down on her hands and knees, bowing and shouting "I'm not worthy! I'm not worthy!" over and over again. I didn't have much respect for Raven to start with but now...

Anyhow, Leslie took in the scene with a little bit of bemusement at first, until boredom and anger finally set in her face. Then she said: "Oh, for fudge's sake! Get up!"

They did.

"Sit down!" she said, pointing to the table.

They did that, too. I could never get people to do that in a million years.

She wanted to grab an extra chair from the table, but the others wanted her to take over my job, since, obviously, she was much more qualified to lead than I was.

"Hello?" I reminded them. "Didn't you guys elect me for the leadership job?"

"Don't be a sore loser, Heather," Raven said, in a tone that told me the request for Leslie to lead was non-negotiable. The look of the other girls was the same. So I was out, just like that.

"You'll regret this!" I shouted, and left the room.

LESLIE'S STORY

Let me level with you, to begin with. We are all victims of an evil plot.

You all know by now why you ended up here. The hatred of America for you, simply because they know not who you are. I know that pain and hatred, too, for I am one of you. I am not a human being, in the conventional sense. I am a cartoon character, and like it or not, so are all of you.

Now, don't start crying or bemoaning your fate. I did that already, and it did me no good.

We can't do anything about the past. All we can be in charge of is the future.

I know you all are surprised to see me here. I'm a little surprised myself.

But not as surprised to learn that nearly my entire life has been captured on film, without my acknowledgement or permission, by people I do not know, who have profited from this - many times over! You, too, have been placed in this situation. Look at any search engine, put a familiar name or phrase in, and you will find portions of our lives on DVDs and in books- for sale! Our exploits, as well, are debated and discussed endlessly on social media. Including speculations on whether or not we would be good friends, or, heaven forbid, lovers.

And it's not just we girls. It's everybody. Powerful or weak, male or female, we are all treated exactly the same way by powerful people who do not understand us- and never will!. And we have to use that sameness to our advantage.

***

The reason my family and I were not part of that savage sweep with the SuperSucker was because they got us before they got you. To my shock and amazement, our show is such an enormously popular cultural phenomenon that you cannot possibly imagine, the government determined to eliminate us first before they took care of you. Overnight, the entire town of Springboard was placed on a contraption called a spin-dizzy, which allows a piece of land to become as mobile in space as any common asteroid. As far as I know, it's orbiting out there still, and I don't know when it's coming back.

My father would not stand for this, seeing he has a very fragile ego, and typically saw the spin-dizzy action as an affront. Somehow or another, he got hold of a space ship, and convinced us all that we could fly back down to Earth. He thought he could convince the people we were real and put the town back on Earth. I don't know why he thought that idea would work, but that's neither here nor there. The trouble was, he misread the word "launch" on the dashboard for "lunch" in one of his weaker moments.

You can imagine the rest.

Point is, we made it here to Orthicon alive, just as the ship ran out of fuel. Fortunately, I'd been following your case on my cell phone all this time, so I know the ins and outs of this thing perfectly. And, since you seem convinced that I'm the person to lead this thing, I'll gladly do it.

But I need something to eat first. You'd be surprised how long I've gone without food.

THE JOURNAL OF TEO TOTINO

June 2——.

I was struck dumb when I saw him there. It couldn't be him.

Baron Stinson. A fictional character whom I'd seen on TV for years. Here. On Orthicon.

"Hey, man," he said, in his trademark laconic way, running a hand through his spiky hair. "You know where I could find someplace to rest? I need a nap."

I pointed, without saying a word (since I couldn't say a thing), in the direction of our base camp.

"Thanks, man," he said. And then he walked off.

I am officially losing my MIND!

THE JOURNAL OF FRANCES SNEAD

June 2—-.

I was getting coffee in the cafeteria when it happened.

The doors are locked from the outside now, since nobody comes in that way anymore. You can only open them from the inside, and that's how it happened.

Somebody was knocking on the outside door.

"Hello?" It was a man, with a rough, sandpaper voice, though softened some by regular use. "Anybody home?"

I rushed to the door, pushed it open, and...

Well, I can't explain it. Harold Stinson- a fictional character- was standing there, his bald head gleaming in the rare shine of Orthiconian sunlight, and his unshaven face, as always, displaying both his limited intelligence and his rakish charm.

"Thanks," he said. "You work here?"

"Uh..." I had been stunned into catatonia.

"Well, thanks for getting the door opened, anyway. There's, like,

nobody here right now! You guys having a long weekend or something?"

"Uh..."

He rushed to the door and opened it. "Meryl!" he shouted.

"What?" an equally familiar sandblast of a voice said.

"This place is open! C'mon!"

"Don't'cha think we should start looking for the kids?"

"They'll manage. They said so, and you know what they're like. Probably doing better than we are right now. C'mon!"

And so Meryl Stinson, with her skyscraper of blue hair and green dress, entered the cafeteria. Again, to my astonishment.

"Listen," Harold asked me, "how much have we gotta pay for a meal?"

"Help yourself," I said, dazed. "Like you said, there's nobody here."

Harold let out a whoop and started for the back kitchen. Meanwhile, Meryl placed a $20 American bill in my hand. I hadn't seen one in ages.

"No, no!" she said, when I tried to give it back. "I insist. You've earned it."

I completely agreed.

I.M. STONED'S MONTHLY

May 2——. (Continued from previous excerpt.)

Of course, Basil and Bonnie are two of the luckier funny animals. Many, under the stresses and strains of Orthicon, have either had goodly portions of their brains fried by persistent alcohol and drug abuse, or have reverted to latent criminal tendencies. It is depressing to see many of them in action. Once accustomed to ruling their domains, they have come crashing horrifically down to Earth.

It is hard to miss their insane laughter, rivaling the most blood-curdling cackles to come out of Bedlam in its prime. Their recitations of dirty limericks and songs, their quotations and paraphrases of their old dialogue in a similar fashion, and the endless, pointless fighting and carousing are consistent. Of course, these are a minority; the ones with more intelligence and free will, such as Basil and Bonnie, stay far away from them for a good reason. But, oh, what a contrast!

If the unlikely and disjointed coalition between this group and the other parties of dissidents is to succeed in their aims, the funny animals who have been impaired the most will likely need to be kept in check. But can this really be done? Who knows?

THE PAPERS OF ROCKWELL WALLABY

June 2——.

You'll never believe it. We actually met the Suckerpunch Girls today.

Of course, Heflin and I knew about 'em by reputation, and they us. Before things went south in Orthicon, we funny animals knew what they'd done to Snead's office after he wouldn't let 'em fight the crime that needed fighting, and we got this bad opinion of 'em from that. Snead had even gone putting up WANTED posters of 'em up all along the telephone posts and everything. Anyone who went near them, they said, was risking getting their arse whipped badly.

So naturally, we were afraid when we saw them flying over, and we started cowering.

They got down and spoke to us.

"WHAT are you doing?" the redhead demanded.

We explained what had happened. Their jaws dropped in horror.

"That's nonsense!" the redhead said. "We don't mean anyone harm unless they're evil."

"And you're not, right?" the brunette asked.

We nodded. "No."

"Oh, come on!" the blonde said. "They're harmless."

"Well, we can't be sure," the redhead said. "Remember that pamphlet the kids were handing around..."

"What pamphlet?" I asked.

They did the explaining, now. Apparently, we funny animals were not to be touched or approached in any way, otherwise the people who touched them would get ebola, swine flu, bird flu, dandruff, Covid-19, and a million and one other diseases, all at once!

"That's as bloody ridiculous as you going 'round beatin' up people at will," I said.

"So there's no truth in it?" the redhead asked.

"If you don't believe us," Heflin said, "touch us!"

They did. Nothing happened. Even kissing us didn't do anything to them. So they were convinced, and we parted ways, pals.

"I think this unity thing is gonna work out between us different groups, eh, Heflin?"

"Aw, yeah, man!" he said. "They can touch and kiss me anytime they want!"

AUDIO LOG OF JANEY WICKMAN

June 2——.

Heather came to me after Leslie Stinson usurped her.

"How could they do this to me?" she asked. "I thought we were friends!"

"Well..." I said.

"If you go along with them and let her lead, I'll kick your ass."

"I'm the one who kicks asses for a living, remember?"

She remembered.

"She seems like a nice enough person," I continued.

"Have you met her? I mean, personally?"

"Actually..." I said, "I haven't."

"Then how do you know she's going this for the greater good? Like I was going to?"

"I know her from television," I said. "Just like you, and everyone else. And that Leslie Stinson is not only an intelligent person, but a kind and just one. Undoubtedly, this one is, too."

She had no response. She was starting to get it, now.

"I think all we can do is do it the way she wants," I concluded.

"You mean, follow her orders?"

"Not orders. Suggestions. Your father was the one who gave orders-and look where it got him."

"I hadn't thought of it like that," she said, and lapsed into silence again.

JOURNAL OF MUCK FLECKNOE

June 2——.

Man! I haven't been able to keep a journal for so long here. After I lost my old notebook, and everything blew up in everybody's faces, somehow things like that didn't seem so important.

I had no supporters, no help, no nothing in the compound. Certainly not that back stabbing imaginary friend of mine. After the Dildo went up, he wouldn't even TALK to me anymore! He made a buttload of money, and wouldn't even give me a small loan.

Not that I asked for one, but still...

Of course, I lapsed into the old ice cream soda addiction, and that did me no good. One day, I was pulling 'em back in the cafeteria. Then, the next thing I knew, I was surrounded by this big bunch of sadistic girls no older than me, and...

No! That injustice perpetrated on my body and soul is unprintable!!!

The point is I got back to Orthicon, alive.

There was nobody there. Even the Orthiconians seemed to have abandoned the place. All I could see in the streets were a bald headed man and a bespectacled fat man who were both sloshed and singing dirty songs. Fearing for my safety, I headed into the Steam Powered Dildo.

There, I ran into two other sloshed guys. Sam Snead, the reprobate consul who got us all into this mess, and my ex-buddy-for-life and (metaphysical) spawn of my loins, Bootylicious J. Krinkelbein. Neither of them was in a position to do much, so I did it for them. I went over and swatted Boot on the side of his head. It wasn't any way to get revenge, but in some small fashion, I got it.

"Oh," Boot said, as soon as he saw me. "It's you!"

"Yeah," I said. "It's me."

"What d'ya want?" Snead drawled.

"Keep it shut, you old fart!" I snapped. "This is between me and him!"

"Ah, c'mon, Muck," Boot drawled. "Keep it down. I got a headache."

"You have the nerve to complain about a headache? And you tell me to keep it down?"

"You heard what he said," Snead chipped in, mustering what was left of his authority.

I kicked Snead, and he went away from the place, leaving me with Boot, alone.

"Give me one good reason," I said, "why I shouldn't do that to you."

"Well," he said, trying to think of something (not very hard).

"I knew it! You don't appreciate me. You never did!"

In a rage, I ran towards the jukebox in the corner.

"I never should have created you!" I declared, angrily.

"Don't say that!" he protested.

Miraculously, he had thrown off a goodly percentage of his inebriation. How, I didn't know or care.

"Come on, Muck!" he said. "We had some good times."

"Name one."

"Uh..."

"Aha!"

At this point, my flare for the dramatic betrayed me. I did not notice that I had placed my hand directly above the glass top of the jukebox. When I said, "Aha!", I dropped my hand down with such force that I broke the top- and my hand- in the process.

"ARGH!" I shouted.

"MUCK!" Boot replied.

Slowly, blood was coagulating over my hand.

But it wasn't colored red, like you would expect.

It was black.

Like ink.

I remembered something I had overheard somebody say. That we weren't like human beings at all, any of us, on Orthicon. Our blood was ink, our skin was paint, and our skeletal structure was celluloid.

They were right about us.

We weren't human.

We were never human to begin with.

It wasn't 'til then that I believed them.

Boot had fetched a towel from the bar, which he fashioned into a tourniquet for my hand. He was genuinely remorseful, much more so than he'd been since we arrived in Orthicon, and even more humane than he'd been before then. For an imaginary friend, he was starting to become more real all the time.

We spent the hours that followed together, reminiscing and arguing- good-naturedly this time- about which one of us was the bigger fool for getting trapped in the unreal vortex of Orthicon, and which of us was more responsible for betraying the other.

It wasn't home, but it was close enough. And it was getting closer all the time.

CHAPTER NINE

Highlights from The Destruction Of Any Sense Of Moral Order

THE WORLD AT SIX, CBC RADIO

June 2———.

...(Music and dialogue in background) The latest Internet sensation is hardly what could be called something of terrestrial origin. It originates from the planet Orthicon, where the so-called cartoon characters of Earth have been in forced encampment since January of this year. Long standing disputes regarding voracious over-control of the colony and the avaricious personal aims of those in charge came to a head in the spring, with rebellious dissidents angrily quitting the colony for their own settlements. Earlier this month, they began releasing a series of videos of YouSuck, all of which have gone viral in spectacular fashion, and all of which angrily voice their complaints in word and song, and in which they promise, later this month, to hold a "picnic" in which they will have a final reckoning with those who have oppressed them.

The American government has refused to make any public comment, on the colony or the reasons for its existence, since news of its existence was first disclosed to the public in April.

FROM I.M. STONED'S MONTHLY

July 2———.

"We want out! We want out! We want out!"

The cry echoed over hill and dale, barren desert, artificial field, artificial stream, and half-built plank building alike as those angered and dismayed by their unjust treatment at the hands of the rapacious American government made themselves known. Holding placards, and chanting the buzzword slogan they had devised to reflect their anger, frustration and fury in a manageable sound bite for the vacuous terrestrial media to get, they gathered en masse to air grievances already known to them, but other than those who have seen them on the Internet, invisible to the world at large.

They were thinking, perhaps, that they were staging another attempt for a minority group at war with a hateful majority to express its sentiments in a peaceful setting.

What they got, instead, was their frustrations denied, and like so many in the past, they took it out on the place they were forced to live- and the beings governing it.

Here is what happened:

A central platform had been erected for speeches and the like some time earlier at the boundaries of the terraformed compound and the barren desert around it, and it was here around which the throng gathered. I was among the throng, in my funny animal disguise, and witnessed the events first hand, I can assure you. Use that as a bluff against anyone who questions the veracity of my report.

Heather Snead, estranged daughter of embattled U.S. consul Sam, took the stage for twentyminutes of inspired rhetoric that, while largely an exercise in preaching to the choir, was still very inspiring. The highlight was leading the crowd in a recitation of I Am Somebody. This is the very same empowerment chant popularized by Reverend Jesse Jackson among African Americans in the 1970s, but Snead and her associates have clearly adapted it for their own purposes:

"I may be a figment of someone's imagination, but I am Somebody!"

"I may have ink in my veins, but I am Somebody!"

"I may be a 'graven image', but I am Somebody!"

"I may not have control of my own destiny, but I am Somebody!"

"I may be someone or something you utterly despise, someone you don't even think is worthy of your attention, but I am Somebody!"

And so on, and so on, and so on.

The volume on the public address system had been turned to the highest possible level, an ear-splitting 11, so that every possible word could be heard in every part of the immediate vicinity, in the hopes that Consul Snead would hear and respond.

He certainly did.

Midway through the "I Am Somebody" liturgy, he became visible, accompanied by the various members of the Executive Defense Committee. Snead himself carried a snub-nosed pistol with the gravity of a Wild West lawman; the others carried weapons- nightsticks, bats, guns, etc.- which they waved threateningly.

Mounting the platform from behind, they overwhelmed those who had been assigned guard duty and hijacked the ceremony, to the growing displeasure of the audience when they began to realize what was going on.

Snead pushed his daughter away from the microphone and ordered the crowd to disperse, which they refused to do

"Then you are all under arrest," he said.

"No," Heather Snead said, pushing him away. "You are. Or you will be, when we get home. And you want to know the worst part? You're a 'toon as much of the rest of us are. You aren't any better, and you never were!"

Cheers from the audience.

"What are you talking about?" Sam Snead said.

"Look at THIS!" Heather produced a DVD package, whose cover she shoved in Sam's face. "Is that not you? Is that not me? Is that not what used to be our family?"

He had no immediate response.

"All right, you," the ubiquitous bobby-like EDC member accompanying Sam on the platform said to Heather, as she put her gun on Heather's back. "Get!"

Heather whirled around and faced her angrily. The bobby aimed the gun, and fired...

...and the bullet passed directly through Heather Snead's body.

'Toons, you must know, are immune to all the works of man. Disease, physical violence, and especially weapons such as firearms. Especially firearms, considering that their bodies are not solid enough for bullets to make an impact on their vital organs.

They have but one weakness. Fire. As image-based bodies, they contain an inner core of nitrate, an inherited condition from years of film production and reproduction over the years in which they were conceived. One spare stroke of flame from something as insignificant as a match can utterly destroy them. That is why I saw no campfires in the hills around Orthicon, nor any roaring fireplaces anywhere in the luxurious hotel-like dorms.

Nor was I to see any flames in the chaos that followed.

No successful attempt had been on Heather Snead's life, but symbolically, the action of firing a bullet at- and through- her was a massive, collective affront to the crowd. With ferocious, unrestrained rage, the 'toons swarmed the platform.

Attempts by the EDC and Snead to defend themselves were futile, as they had exactly the wrong kind of weapons. They were soon driven away, save for Sam Snead himself, who seemed to be held as some sort of hostage by some disaffected members of the group.

They roared into the compound, disassembling the buildings at a faster rate than they had been originally constructed, accompanying their wanton acts with ferocious, baying howls and profanity-laden tirades. They forced themselves inside any building they could manage and drove whomever they could find out at the point of their weapons. It was not something everyone participated in- some, including myself, openly declined- but those who did took a l relish in it which was utterly horrifying to see.

When the compound was officially declared wrecked, they began, suddenly, to turn on each other. Old sectional, gender and species differences in ideology and politics reasserted themselves with a vengeance. With tempers already broken, they fought with each other, verbally and physically, blaming each other for what they had done to Orthicon instead of admitting they'd done it to themselves. Physical violence ultimately took precedence over the verbal kind, in ways even professional wrestling officials would not consider legal means, and the scene degenerated even further into anarchy. The bodies displayed black eyes, torn hair and disheveled clothing, but they seemed to have no lack of energy to fight.

The physical strength and endurance possessed by these beings is far greater than any mere human being, and utterly remarkable. When under control, it is immensely useful. When not, it is destructive in the worst sense imaginable.

Ultimately, however, things came to an end.

Ms. Leslie Stinson- who has become the de facto leader of the rebels since her arrival in the colony a spare two months ago- came upon the scene.

That she was shocked and appalled by what she saw was immediately evident when I happened to see her face. No words could fully convey the level of anger that was evident in it. None were needed.

It was the kind of anger that, like that of the feuding 'toons, needed a proper outlet. Unlike theirs, it found one, and immediately.

She ascended the raised platform and grasped the abandoned microphone. She pulled an air-horn from the pocket of her red dress, pressed the horn against the microphone, and pulled the horn's trigger.

Immediately, a loud sound created from the combination of the horn and the microphone/speaker feedback- a sort of HWAAAAAAAA/WHEAAAAAAWWWW- staggered across the compound, causing all in hearing distance to grasp their ears in pain, and some to crumble into fetal positions, as if they were back in their wombs.

They turned their eyes to where the sound came from, saw her electric blue eyes glaring at them in a way that demanded immediate and compliant silence, and were shamed into giving it to them, and she whirled around and spoke into the microphone.

"I am thoroughly disgusted with you! We had a plan for doing this the right way, and you blew it! How can we possibly achieve the respect and citizenship I know you all want, when you decide to behave like pig-headed idiots whenever you get the chance?!

"Of course, it's not all your fault. Much of it has to do with your faulty and biased management, of which you are well aware. But, if you are not prepared to behave in a civilized way that will allow you to gain respect, you will not receive such treatment in return. That is a statement of fact which is undisputable.

"You all want to return to your lives as they were before you came. That is simply impossible. The worlds from which we came are no more. They were destroyed by the U.S. government after we were evacuated from them. And even if they were restored to us intact, the personal and psychological toll upon is too great for a full restoration of our old ways of living to be achieved. We are not the beings we used to be, and we will never be those creatures again. It is futile for us to think otherwise.

"All we can do is resume lives governed as much by normalcy as possible- providedwe get back to Earth!

"Now, here is what I want you to do. Go into those dormitories, lie down on the beds, and rest. Even if you don't fall asleep, think about what you did while you were here, especially today, and how you can possibly atone for it in the eyes of the world."

With that, she dropped the microphone, and approached Snead, who was cowering impotently on the ground nearby.

"I want you," she told him, coldly, "to tender your resignation as Consul, and request ships to come here ASAP to return us to Earth."

"Well," he said evasively, "I need to..."

She put a death grip on his throat with her yellow-skinned hands, in a surprising show of strength.

"I don't mean in an hour, or tomorrow." She growled, loudly. "I mean now!"

She let him go, and he ran away.

Thus did the events of the day come to an end.

PERSONAL DIARIES OF THE SUCKERPUNCH GIRLS

FLOTSAM:

"Hello, ladies," he purred. "Did you enjoy the spectacle?"

We whirled around to see that little bald-headed guy who'd flirted with Baubles when we first got here, his arms folded in a confident gesture. Like he had a secret he wanted us to pry out of him. We were sure going to do that.

"I should say we didn't!" I told him. "Did you see what happened? It was a rampage of horrible proportions. Even we were powerless to stop it!"

"I did. And I must say, it all went according to my plan."

We were staggered into silence for a moment.

"Your plan?" I said, disbelievingly.

BETTERFIST:

"Exactly," he retorted. "My plan."

"What, exactly, was your plan?" I demanded, putting a fist in a palm.

"My plan was to humble all of you. Get you to understand that your worlds were fictional, and easily destroyed. I saw all of you, arrogantly prancing around the cathode rays, immune to all passions and temptations of the 'real' world. You needed to learn how to experience things for real, as it were."

"And you were the one who made it happen," Flotsam said. "Not the government?"

"Oh, they did all the heavy lifting for me. I merely pushed the straw onto the camel's back."

"How?" I demanded.

"I sent an e-mail to President Mucklebackit, telling him all about you and your kind, and how you needed to be destroyed. How your flagrant liberalism was an affront to the deeds he hoped to do in a purely conservative America, where everyone does what they're told and no one questions anything told to them. My kind of place."

"You do realize," Flotsam said, "that you're one of us."

"That, I only came to realize as you did, during my abduction. It hadn't been something I had planned for. But it gave me the advantage of falling in love."

"With who?" I said.

"Who do you think?" he answered.

BAUBLES:

"Me!" I said. "You fell in love with me, right?"

"Yes, darling," he said. "But I knew, with your sisters opposing the match, it wasn't to be. So that was why I came to Snead and convinced you that your super heroism had to be controlled."

"What?" we growled.

"You heard me. Because you have super powers, you're a cut above the other 'toons, even though most of us are pretty super to begin with. And you had to be humbled."

"So you were the one who turned us into shadows of who we used to be!"

I snapped, my temper gone.

"It was worth it, to get you into my arms, child" he said, opening his arms for an embrace that would never happen.

"Child?" I ran over to him- and punched him right between the eyes. Screaming, he flew backwards in the air, until his body crashed somewhere out in the desert. Then I ran back to Flotsam and Betterfist, who held me sympathetically.

"It's all right, Baubles. Everything's going to be fine from now on."

We could only hope it would be.

RESIGNATION LETTER OF SAM SNEAD, CONSUL, ORTHICON

I, Samson J. Snead, hereby resign the consulship of Orthicon, effective at noon tomorrow, and request a fleet of ships to come to Orthicon to retrieve the populace and return them to settlements of their choice on Earth.

I admit that I have grievously abused my position, in the process estranging myself permanently from the affections of those I governed, including my family. I operated purely on a flawed methodology that assumed that all 'toons were one and the same, and that if they were treated with what I considered to be discipline, they would fall in line and behave, as those who assigned me this post naively and ignorantly assumed that they would. Time and politics have proven otherwise.

I am prepared to accept any criminal charges that may be proffered against me on Earth for my actions, for I know, in my heart, I have broken many laws of the land in the benign assumption that they did not apply out here in space. I can vouch that many of my colleagues in the Executive Defense Committee did the same, which resulted in the chaotic state of affairs that resulted on Orthicon. However, they did so only and entirely under my orders, so I will accept full responsibility for the way they conducted themselves.

I recognize also, now, that I am not a "pure" human being, but a 'toon, and am attempting to reconcile myself to this. It will not be an easy process.

Finally, I wish to convey to you that the planet Orthicon is now in a state of war with the U.S. government. They have no means to attack Earth directly, but I am assured, if any being of Earth ever comes to the planet again, they will be shot and killed on sight, without any prior warning.

Sincerely,

[Signature]

Samson J. Snead

United States Consul, Orthicon

CHAPTER TEN

Going Home

THE JOURNAL OF BRENDAN GUTMAN

July 2——.

"Is this seat taken?" she said.

I looked away from my book, and there she was. My ex-girlfriend.

" Cad!" I exclaimed.

We canine 'toon citizens of Earth were preparing to leave Orthicon on board the spaceship, in accordance with the terms of our dispersal from the abandoned colony. Because of the raucousness that had climaxed our stay, the government, in its limited wisdom, decided to separate us in terms of race, as we had been during our stay on the planet. We had a few minutes left before our very fast paced flight to Earth was to begin.

Cad was looking a bit downtrodden, so I invited her to sit next to me, and she obliged.

"I want you to know," she said, as she buckled up, "that I am truly sorry for what I said to you, and I wish to attempt a reconciliation."

"What did you say to me?" I asked.

"Oh, you know- about the Black Panthers."

"What?" I'd forgotten that, so she reminded me.

"Remember? What you said about them?

"Yeah?"

"You were right. I knew them only by image, not by reputation. So, after we had our little spat, I went into Orthicon and used one of those blasted e-readers to look them up on Wikiwacky."

"That's not the most reliable source," I reminded her.

"It was all we had there, remember? Anyway, everything you said was true."

"I had no reason to doubt that it wasn't."

We both contemplated our futures, with beaming grins, as the ship zoomed its way home.

EDITOR'S CONCLUSION

What you have just read is only a small portion of the available literature on Orthicon, compiled as best as possible from the sources to provide you with a picture of what occurred there. Any one of the multiple narrators presented here could have told you a complete story with their full annotations and records. However, in the interest of narrative balance, and to avoid bias, I have tried to cherry-pick a record from the available notes in such a way that the variances in personality, politics, attitude and other such things in the record are noticeable, and prevent one narrative from being dominant among all the rest. I hope sincerely that this has been accomplished.

My hope is that this presentation will encourage further scholarship of 'toon issues, of which this serves as the true, essential starting point. Orthicon was their Great Awakening, and all future incidents of striving for 'toon rights- from the Great Rebellion in Gary to the formation and activities of the Cartoon Republican Army, both of which have previously been analyzed- will stand a better chance of being fully understood in an objective context, away from the biased, exaggerated, and highly racist context under which their aims, ideals and desires are presented by the mainstream mass media.

'Toons, whatever form they take among us, are exactly what they pretend to be. And that, then and especially now, is all that we should expect them to be.

About the Author

David Perlmutter is a freelance writer based in Winnipeg, Manitoba, Canada. He is the author of two books on animation history: America 'Toons In: A History of Television Animation (McFarland and Co.) and The Encyclopedia Of American Animated Television Shows (Rowman and Littlefield), as well as essays and works of speculative fiction..

9 798223 239222

Printed by Libri Plureos GmbH in Hamburg, Germany